Sir John Averill knew that sooner or later he would have to introduce his two wards, Vinca and Syn, to the upperair world. It was as much their right, their heritage, as was the sea in which they had lived with him and his dolphins ever since they had been babies.

Still, he was reluctant to expose them in all their naivetee and innocence. Consequently, when Averill brought his two young savages to London, he hedged them about with protective devices—chief among these being the sophisticated guidance of the worldly Duchess of Beaux.

The Duchess, however, proved to be no bulwark against the wide-eyed, avid curiosity of the two girls whose uninhibited questions on every subject under the sun left her exhausted—and frequently shocked. Nor could she hope to control Syn and Vinca when they were on their own.

Indeed, Syn and Vinca, although they learned fast, fairly shook the "civilized" humans they encountered with the directness of their approach. And humans generally don't like being shook.

They quickly got into trouble—indeed, some of their troubles became actively dangerous. At which point, Triton, Sir John Averill, decided he'd better take a hand again—and found himself longing for the simple days when the only problem to be coped with might be a hungry shark. . .

Other titles by Roy Meyers

THE DOLPHIN BOY
DAUGHTERS OF THE DOLPHIN

Also available in Ballantine Books.

This is an original publication—not a reprint

DESTINY AND THE DOLPHINS

Roy Meyers

BALLANTINE BOOKS • NEW YORK

*This book is dedicated
to my charming nieces
Clare and Fay Meyers*

Here at the quiet limit of the world.
　　　　　　　—Tennyson

DESTINY AND THE DOLPHINS

Roy Meyers

chapter one

MY FAIR LADY was a fifty-foot luxury cabin cruiser. She was fitted with every kind of modern equipment, including an echo sounder and radiotelephone. It had been a fine day and she was traveling at maximum speed toward her destination, the Firth of Forth. Off the coast of Northumberland she ran into bad weather which developed into a northeasterly gale. One of her twin diesels chose this inappropriate moment to sputter to stillness, leaving her with only one engine which was inadequate in the heavy seas and driving wind of the northeaster. In spite of all the skipper could do the howling wind blew her steadily inshore until her bows were driven into a sandbank. Reversing the engine did not free her and she lay trapped and pounded by mountainous waves. A distress rocket was fired and a slender young man began to transmit on the distress wave of 1650 kilocycles. He was in luck for it was only a few minutes off the hour. For the first three minutes of each hour all transmission must cease in the bands between 1630 and 1670 kilocycles while

1

stations of the mobile service who are in radio contact with ships of low tonnage listen. Within a short time he was in communication with the nearest coast-guard station.

A white open Maserati with coachwork by Ghibli raced down the coast road toward Blythe. As 5000 r.p.m. came up on the tachometer, the blonde flicked the short stubby gear lever into top and the four twin-choke Weber carburetors thrust the car forward with ever-increasing speed. Her hair was whipped back by the wind and she reveled in the elements as the car hurtled along the empty road. On her left sand dunes led down to a tumultuous sea and she took a deep breath of salty air. The wind howled, the sea roared and she had the sensation of being alone between earth and sky. She could see Holy Island in the distance battered by huge white waves, and then farther along the coast she had a sudden view of the cabin cruiser. As she drew near she saw a small group of windswept men standing on the shore around a triangular erection. She slowed the car as one of them fired a rocket. A thin line snaked through the air, fighting against the inshore wind. She pulled up behind some other cars and watched as it fell short and was hauled in.

"The damn wind's too strong," said a burly coast guard.

"It may ease up suddenly."

The big man grunted skeptically.

"We'll keep trying until she breaks up," he said.

"Which won't be long in this sea," replied his companion.

The slender girl got out of the car and slamming

the door behind her, walked down the dunes, leaning forward and pushing her way against the wind.

One of the coast guards saw her and nudged his companion.

"Look what's coming."

His friend gave a whistle of appreciation which was blown away but a young man dressed in tweeds heard the remark and looked at the approaching girl who, even in the gale, crossed the sand with a peculiar grace. She reached the group of men as they fired another rocket without success. Syn suddenly saw a dense plume of white smoke rise from the sea.

"What's that?" she asked.

"It's a flare on a lifebuoy, miss."

Synclaire Phelan looked at the coast guard.

"They're trying to float a line ashore," he added.

Green eyes regarded him thoughtfully.

"Will it get here?" she asked.

"Not in time, miss. She'll break up before then, poor devils."

"It's not far away," she said, looking at the ship.

"It could be a hundred miles from land for all the difference it'll make," said the young man in tweeds bitterly.

Syn looked at Antony Watson for the first time. He was a beautiful young man, she thought, and felt the color rise in her face. They stood gazing at each other and Antony suddenly realized she was the loveliest creature he had ever seen.

"Surely they can swim ashore," she said transferring her gaze with an effort back to the ship.

The coast guard had retrieved the nylon cord which now lay neatly coiled at his feet. He straightened up with a grunt and gazed curiously at the girl.

"Nothing could live in this sea, miss," he said shortly.

Syn turned to him in surprise.

"It will be quiet enough below the surface."

Her remark was met by silence.

"What will happen to the crew?" she said.

The burly man shrugged his shoulders.

"There's a lifeboat on the way, let's hope it gets here in time."

"Will it?" she asked bluntly.

He coughed and rubbed his chin.

"I doubt if she'll last that long. She wasn't made for this kind of treatment."

"Can you save them if you get the rope aboard?" asked Syn.

She was an attractive creature and the coast guard sighed patiently instead of giving a sharp retort.

"We ain't firing rockets for fun, miss." He pointed to the tripod of spars with tail block hanging from the apex. "We hoped to fix up a breeches buoy and haul them ashore."

"I'll take the line out for you," said the girl calmly.

The other men had gathered round and the remark was received in silence except for one of them who looked at the sea and sniggered.

"It's a brave offer but you'd only drown," said Antony Watson soothingly.

Syn looked at the faces round her.

"I'll swim beneath the surface."

"You'll never get out, miss," said the big coast guard kindly.

"Tie the rope round my waist and if I get into

trouble you can haul me in—I'm going anyway," she said and began to peel off her clothes.

"Here now, wait a minute—" the coast guard began to expostulate.

Antony stepped forward in an attempt to stop such foolishness but was brushed peremptorily aside. The men stood round not knowing what to do.

In very short order she stood slim and graceful in panties and bra. There was a concerted effort not to gape.

"Well?" she said.

The cord was tied reluctantly round her slim waist.

"If you should get out there tie this round the lifebuoy," said the coast guard, quite certain they would shortly be hauling in an exhausted and half-drowned girl, but a jolly plucky one he thought. Nothing would make him try to swim in such a sea.

"If you get tired raise an arm above your head and we'll pull you in," he added.

She smiled and looking slim and defenseless walked toward the sea, the nylon cord trailing behind her like an umbilical cord. She hesitated as a great wave broke and rushed up the sand and then as it was sucked back she darted after it and dived cleanly through the next breaker as it curled high above her head. She reveled in the return to her native element and hugged the ocean bed for the water was not very deep. Arms to her side and her legs close together with feet everted she thrust her way powerfully through the sea as the dolphins had taught her. Muscular contractions rippled almost unseen down her body and as she picked up speed and fled through the sea, she wondered what Triton and

5

Vinca were doing. The men stood watching anxiously and it was Antony who first noticed the nylon
cord.

"Look at it," he shouted in surprise.

The big coast guard stared in disbelief as coil after
coil whipped off and vanished into the water.

"She must be going like a bomb," he muttered
and gazed seaward. Only tumultuous waves and broken water met his gaze.

As the length of cord increased its speed diminished but it was still disappearing at a brisk rate.

"She'll be there in a minute at this speed," said the
coast guard unbelievingly and almost before he had
finished speaking the cord slowed and stopped.

"She's reached the buoy," he shouted excitedly.

"How will she get back?" asked Antony.

"The way she went. God! How that girl can swim!
I wonder who the hell she is?"

"The waves will smash her as she comes in,"
Antony said anxiously.

The coast guard shouted orders and the men
strung out along the water's edge waiting and
watching. Their eyes searched each wave as it curled
and crashed down on the sand, and a tenseness
settled over the group. Suddenly there was a shout.

"There she is!"

As Syn approached the shore she surfaced and
swam in on top of a large breaker. They saw a flash
of white limbs and tumble of golden hair and then
she was spewed upon the sand. Before the undertow
could suck her back she was seized by willing hands
and dragged to safety up the beach. She was smiling,
fresh and almost naked and one of the men wrapped

an overcoat about her. There were admiring but hurried congratulations.

"I'll take her to the nearest hotel," said Antony for the coast guards now had work to do. He left them vigorously pulling in the lifebuoy. They could now rig up a breeches buoy and haul the crew to safety but it was imperative that they get them off before the ship foundered. They were fighting against time, and as the girl was obviously all right, the men left her to Antony's care.

Syn's calm green eyes, golden hair and graceful figure had completely captivated Antony. Her cool, detached yet friendly manner charmed him and her inability to consider what she had done as anything out of the ordinary intrigued him. He had never met a girl like her before and was pleased to hear she lived in London.

Syn was equally enamored and admired Antony's dark hair and clean-cut figure. She was delightfully impressed with the way she was treated. He quickly arranged a hot bath, a room for her to change in, and a hot meal before she continued her journey to London. She was returning from a stay with the Cunninghams, and luckily had some clothes with her.

She drank in his obvious admiration. Owing to her unique upbringing this was her first emotional experience with an upper-air male. By the end of their meal together he had arranged to phone her as soon as he got to London. When Syn and Antony eventually separated they were under the impression that they knew each other very well. The symphony of the ductless glands had begun. She wondered what Triton and Vinca would think and looked forward to introducing him, for she was certain they would approve as much as she did.

She had come a long way since leaving the sea for the land, she thought, as she drove toward London and her thoughts returned to the first ship she had ever known, the *Poseidon* and the voyage to England.

Her first sight of the schooner with its towering rigging and white sails had taken her breath away, and as it hissed majestically through the sea she had fallen in love with it. Her first trip on the *Poseidon* had been an experience she would never forget.

A sea mist began to blow up, and she slowed down, driving automatically as her thoughts dwelt on the three-masted topsail schooner, the hot Caribbean sunshine and her two companions, Triton her guardian, and Vinca her twin sister.

chapter two

THE SHIP *Poseidon* plunged through the swells of the Caribbean on her way to Jamaica. The sun shone out of a blue sky laced with fleecy clouds and the three-masted topsail schooner made good time before a following wind. Her speed peeled open the ocean in two white waves and left a creamy wake behind her. She was luxury-built and over ninety feet long with a twenty-foot beam. Only the occasional creak of her rigging could be heard as she hissed majestically through the sea under full sail.

Young Mr. Greenway stood at the wheel loving the job of guiding this beautiful ship as she coursed through the sea. When you hold the wheel of a sailing ship this size the power of her under your hands is a sensation never to be forgotten. He was very conscious of the two lithe girls sunbathing on the poop deck behind him.

When they first came aboard from Crab Island, which was owned by their guardian Sir John Averill, the young sailor had been greatly moved by their grace and beauty. After a day or two he had been

9

reduced almost to a trancelike state and was hardly able to keep his mind on his job when in their vicinity. Syn was a cool blonde and Vinca a vivacious brunette and each was the equal of the other in beauty and seductive appeal.

Sir John Averill looked only a few years older than his wards. Startling blue eyes looked out of a thoughtful aquiline face. The Caribbean sun had tanned his skin brown and bleached his fair hair almost white. His smooth limbs and slender frame belied the steellike strength which could send him hurtling through the seas at nearly thirty knots. He was known as Triton by his few intimates because of his unique history. He had been lost in the Caribbean as a child but due to his peculiar lung construction had survived in the care of dolphins who had taught him to speak their high fluting language and to travel with their speed and dexterity. Both girls had a similar history, thanks to Triton, which explained why they were more at home in the sea than on the land, none of them having walked upon the earth until they were almost adults. Mr. Greenway eventually became accustomed to seeing the three of them casually dive overboard at least once during the day and vanish into the vastness of the ocean. Nothing would be seen of them for several hours until they appeared up the rope ladder that permanently trailed from the stern. Looking fresh and renewed they would dress and continue normal shipboard life as if nothing unusual had happened, which, as far as they were concerned, was in fact the case.

The *Poseidon* continued with unabated speed, the weather remained good and the wind favorable with the result that she made good time, reaching Jamaica early one fine morning.

Oswald Raynor, Triton's first upper-air friend, was getting old and in spite of the sunshine sat with a thin rug over his knees. There was a pair of binoculars on his lap with which he would from time to time search the sea. He picked out the *Poseidon* as soon as she appeared and watched her as she berthed at her moorings. She was a beautiful sight full rigged and he sighed with disappointment. He was a merchant banker, his firm of Raynor & Reynolds had a worldwide reputation. He had financed the research ship of the same name which had netted Triton in the depths of the sea and he had been partly responsible for initiating him into the ways of men and in establishing his identity. He looked forward to seeing Triton again and meeting the girls whom he had only observed for a short period as they cavorted like mermaids below the surface of the lagoon at Crab Island. His mind went back nostalgically over the extraordinary adventures of Triton, adventures in which he had been involved—and he regretted the passing of the years.

Vinca and Syn, under Triton's tutelage, had only recently left the sea and learned to walk upon the land. All three of them had been subjected to prenatal radiation and the resulting change in their development, particularly in the lungs, meant that they could breathe more efficiently and take in three times more air with one breath than normal. Their respiratory rate therefore was very low but not necessarily noticeably so. The glandular formation of their skin, too, was slightly more complex than normal and when in contact with water for any length of time it developed a fine slick of oil invisible to the naked eye. It was these slight differences that enabled them to live in the sea and be successfully adopted and brought up by the dolphins.

When Triton discovered that the two small orphans who were his godchildren were similar to himself he determined they should inherit their birthright, namely the ability to live in the sea and master its environment as he had done. He had taken them into the sea and given them dolphin foster mothers. As they grew up and gradually became independent of their darling dolphins he had taken a hand in their education and development. By the time they reached puberty they could speak Dolphinese fluently and swim with the dolphins' speed and agility. The three of them roamed the ocean hunting and exploring.

They could hardly believe him when he explained they were humans who could live in the upper-air world. Greatly excited, they eventually learned to walk upon the land and explored with delight all the amazing artifacts in his house on Crab Island. They learned to speak the language of men and Triton was now taking them on a world cruise to further their education.

Oswald Raynor thought of all this as he sat in the sun and watched the *Poseidon* drop anchor. It was through him that Vicky, the Duchess of Beaux, was on board to act as chaperone and to teach the girls manners and deportment. She was a beautiful young woman of famous lineage who was both fascinated and delighted with the situation and she had soon made friends with Vinca and Syn.

Oswald Raynor was to have joined the ship which

was calling at Jamaica especially to pick him up but he feared that he was not well enough to go on such a cruise. In the last few weeks he had developed a cough and some shortness of breath. He had been seen by a doctor on the island who had advised him to return to London for a full investigation. Treatment had made no difference, which the doctor had warned him might be the case, so reluctantly he had decided to take the doctor's advice.

Oswald Raynor walked slowly up the gangway to be greeted by Triton.

"It's good to see you again, Oswald," he said observing his friend's slow tread with concern. This was not the brisk bustling little man he had left in London only a few months previously. He took the older man's arm affectionately and led him under the awning which Nero and Hercules had erected as soon as they were berthed. The Duchess of Beaux was presiding over a large silver pot of steaming coffee.

"You're just in time, Oswald."

Raynor smiled at her.

"You're looking as lovely as ever, Vicky," he said sinking gratefully into a chair.

She poured him a cup of black coffee while he, with a certain cussed looked in his eye, lit a cigar. He blew out a streamer of smoke and looked round the deck expectantly.

"Where are they?"

Vicky laughed. "So even you are not immune."

"I'm just curious," said Oswald a little sharply. "The only time I've seen them they were playing about on the bottom of the lagoon and I thought that ghastly octopus was about to kill them." He shuddered reminiscently. "They certainly choose extraordinary playmates," he added acidly.

Vicky glanced at Triton for neither of them had ever seen Oswald so touchy. Before they could answer he had a sudden fit of coughing and by the time he had put away his handkerchief Vinca and Syn were approaching along the deck. Oswald Raynor looked at them with undisguised interest and noticed they walked with the same fluid grace as Triton. Their bodies, tanned brown by the sun, were smooth and shapely yet hid muscles that could send them hurtling through the sea at almost the same speed as their guardian. The result of years of arduous physical training which enabled them to do this showed itself in the smooth flowing movements of their walk.

Oswald Raynor rose as they approached and Triton introduced them. They hesitated shyly and reluctantly shook his outstretched hand. What beautiful creatures they are, thought Raynor, whose view was interrupted only by a pair of minute bikinis. They both gazed at him with interest and an expression he was unable to evaluate—which was just as well. He was the first old person they had seen and neither found his appearance pleasing. Living in the sea, they were unfamiliar with the concept of age and each was unsuccessfully trying to define what she saw. It was continually forgotten during their sojourn among men that they had stepped fully grown as it were from the sea on to the land with the same innocence that Eve must have had before she ate the apple of the tree of knowledge.

Each girl's ability to talk and to behave in a socially acceptable manner, which she had only re-

14

cently learned from Vicky, was a thin veneer over what was basically a wild creature. Their natural habitat was the sea where they depended entirely on themselves. They were familiar with all the ocean's dangers and, unseen by men, they could tear at speed through its watery depths either chasing their prey or fleeing from danger. Oswald Raynor puzzled them and they were faintly repulsed by his shrunken figure and wrinkled skin.

Although a very intelligent woman, the Duchess of Beaux was continually being surprised, not so much at their lack of knowledge for which she was prepared, but at their suddenly revealed and unexpected alien viewpoint. Vinca and Syn were probably the only people who could still, on occasion, shock the duchess. It was a great ordeal for them to enter an alien world full of raucous humans and new concepts which they did not understand and they could never have done it without Triton. With him beside them they felt safe and even when they had learned the rules and manners of society and felt more at home in the upper-air world they always made sure of knowing exactly where he was, so they could reach him quickly if the need arose.

"Are you looking forward to the trip?" asked Triton thinking that the voyage would do his old friend good. He knew he was never so happy as when at sea.

"I was."

Vicky raised her eyebrows. "What does that mean, Oswald?"

"I've not been feeling so well recently and the doctor here has advised against a long sea trip."

"I'm sorry to hear that," said Triton gravely, "has he told you what's wrong?"

"No, but he has advised me to return to London for a checkup."

"What a wicked shame," said Vicky feelingly, "we were so looking forward to your coming. It won't be the same without you, will it, John?"

"It certainly won't. Is there any urgency in getting to England?"

"The doctor didn't say so."

"Then we'll take you home in the *Poseidon*."

"What a good idea," said Vicky enthusiastically for she was very fond of Oswald.

"I'd love it, but what about your trip?" asked Oswald.

"We can start it that way as well as any other," Triton replied easily.

Oswald brightened up.

"I'll get my luggage on board immediately," he said briskly and for a moment they both saw the old Oswald Raynor.

Hercules and Nero brought Raynor's luggage aboard and stowed it in his cabin. Syn and Vinca were dying to go ashore for this was their first sight of civilization. They were astonished at what appeared to them to be the vast number of buildings and the crowds of people.

Triton saw Raynor comfortably settled in, with Hercules helping him to unpack, and then the four of them set off, the girls dancing with excitement.

Vicky was enchanted with their enthusiasm. She was smartly dressed in a neat white linen suit and with her auburn hair and graceful figure was a lovely woman in her own right. The glances of the crowd, however, were directed at the two girls whose beauty and liquid movements immediately caught the eye. To walk almost unnoticed, especially among men, was a new experience for the Duchess of Beaux but she took it in good part with an almost complacent smile on her lips. She felt a proprietary interest in her charges and watched them curiously. This was the first time they had met humanity in the mass and they were either unaware of the interest they were causing or considered it natural. They were both tanned a deep brown and the flaxen-haired beauty of Syn set off the dark loveliness of her sister. Everyone who saw them wondered who they were. They noticed that Triton possessed the same strange grace of movement and mistook them for brother and sisters. The stroll was continually interrupted as the girls halted in surprise or astonishment. They were amazed at the size of the buildings, especially the hotels, having seen only the single-story house on Crab Island which they had always considered enormous. They were fascinated with the numbers of gaily dressed people, particularly children. They had never seen the young of their own species before. They stood still in wonder as a bicycle passed and both clutched Triton's arm at their first sight of a motorcar.

"It's alive," breathed Vinca with wide eyes as it careered down the street blowing its horn. Both girls mistook it for some kind of animal.

"No, it's a little land ship," said Triton.

"What's it for?" asked Syn curiously.

"It saves you walking," said Vicky.

Both girls immediately wanted to go in one and Triton beckoned a taxi.

"Just drive around," he said.

"Yes, sah," said the Jamaican with a wide smile. He engaged gears and rumbled off while the girls sat entranced.

"Faster," said Vinca.

"Yes, ma'am," said the driver in admiration and pushed his foot enthusiastically down on the accelerator. They shot round the island with the driver pointing out sights of interest to his charming fares and after one or two narrow misses an apprehensive Vicky wished he would keep his eyes more on the road and less on his excited passengers.

Vinca turned to Triton.

"Can I try?"

Vicky shut her eyes resignedly. That would be the last straw she thought. It seemed to her more than likely they would end up in a terrible crash as it was. Triton, who had sat impassively during the drive, explained it was impossible and was soon plunged into an explanation of driving licenses and insurance while the driver listened to the conversation in some astonishment. While this was in progress the duchess said to him authoritatively, "Take us to the stores."

"Yes, ma'am," said the driver and flipping the wheel suddenly without giving any apparent sign dived down a turning to the right. Vicky clutched her handbag tightly and considered they would be lucky to get out of the car alive.

"What are stores?" asked Syn.

The car swerved dangerously as the startled driver glanced at her.

"Where you buy things," answered Vicky patiently.

"What's that mean?" asked Vinca temporarily

18

diverted from her attempt to persuade Triton to let her guide this fascinating little ship.

The driver, whose loquaciousness had suddenly stopped, rolled his eyes apprehensively and depressed the accelerator until they were tearing toward the shopping center at a pace that alarmed the duchess.

"Not so fast," she said sharply.

The speed did not diminish.

"Are you deaf?" said Triton ominously.

"No, sah," said the Jamaican and reluctantly reduced his speed.

He pulled up at the first store and the four of them got out. Syn took Vicky's left arm and Vinca her right.

"Show us," they said almost in the same breath.

The three of them strolled along while the amused Triton followed. Both girls were fascinated and could only be persuaded to leave one store in order to enter another equally full of amazing treasures. They watched people taking away their purchases and assumed you helped yourself to whatever you wanted and they were delighted. They had not yet been introduced to the concept of money.

Each began to choose things, silk scarfs, bangles, necklaces, a small red leather purse and a host of other things until Vicky looked at Triton helplessly.

"I believe they think it's all free," she said.

"I'm sure they do but let's not spoil the pleasure of their first experience."

"Can they take what they like then?"

"Certainly, I'll get a boy to carry their spoils to the ship," he said.

Syn and Vinca spent a glorious afternoon which they never forgot.

"I'll see their tutor starts teaching them about money immediately," said the duchess as they returned to the *Poseidon* but Triton only laughed.

The next morning the *Poseidon* again made for the open sea but her original plans were changed and her destination was now London. This meant she would pass between the islands of Cuba and Hispaniola and enter the northwestern Atlantic basin. She would cross the Nares Deep and eventually the mid-Atlantic Ridge to enter the northeastern Atlantic basin opposite the shores of Spain and France. Then rounding Brest and Cherbourg she would enter the English Channel.

Triton called the girls up to the chartroom.

"I want to show you where we are going."

A map was pinned on the board and he had marked their course with a line in red ink.

"We are here," he said pointing to Jamaica, "and we follow this line until we reach England." Maps were still a mystery to them and they looked at it in surprise.

"It's no distance at all," said Vinca.

"On the contrary its a very long way, about five thousand miles in a straight line."

Syn put out her hand and disdainfully spanned the distance between her thumb and little finger.

"How can it be so far?" she said.

Triton suddenly remembered himself asking Oswald the same question when he had been in such a hurry to meet Della and had been shown the distance on a map.

Syn tapped his shoulder.

"Wake up," she said looking at him curiously.

He smiled and began to explain the apparent mystery. During a pause Vinca interrupted. They had a tutor on board, a learned middle-aged scholar who fought valiantly against his charming pupils' erratic ways.

They had him under their pretty thumbs and it was their own eagerness for knowledge that made them learn rather than any discipline Dr. Guise attempted to exert.

"We have been learning about money," said Vinca.

"A strange subject," added Syn.

Vinca colored.

"We had no idea," she said.

"Vinca means did we use too much in Jamaica?" said Syn. Triton felt his heart warm toward these two as they regarded him anxiously.

"What I have is yours," he said simply. "I don't think you could spend too much," he added thoughtfully, "but if you do I'll tell you."

They felt reassured and listened with concentration to his explanation of maps.

The weather remained perfect and the sun shone out of a cloudless sky as they made for the Windward Passage between Cuba and Hispaniola. At least once every day Triton would dive overboard while the ship continued imperturbably on her way, and the two girls always accompanied him. They kept a close watch and when he disappeared into his cabin they hurried to their own. Here they would slip into their metal briefs and brassieres which Triton had specially designed for them. They were made of a fine metal mesh that was as pliable as silk and the golden alloy was unaffected by sea water. Its weight exactly counterbalanced them in the sea so that if necessity demanded they could become immobile like fish and neither rise nor sink.

They reappeared on deck like two graceful goddesses, the metal scintillating in the sun against their brown skin. Triton, similarly attired, looked like Apollo ready to drive his sun steeds across the sky. A razor-sharp dagger was incorporated in his shorts and because of his greater weight he wore knuckle-dusters covered with wicked-looking spikes which made his fists, when clenched, into lethal weapons. Without appearing to notice them he ran and dived over the stern and entered the water with a girl on either side of him. They plunged down deep, bubbles streaming from their hair and surprised fish scattering before them. They fled through the sea at top speed reveling in the play of their muscles and in the freedom of their natural habitat. Triton was in the lead as custom demanded, with a girl equally spaced on either side of him, their heads at the level of his shoulders. They swam with the speed and grace of the dolphins who had taught them, their arms to their sides, their legs straight and tight together with feet everted. The sea floor flew beneath them and they turned and twisted as one.

"This is the only way to travel," piped Vinca in the high-pitched fluting tones of Dolphinese. They fled tirelessly through the sea with a slight undulating movement of their bodies as a ring of muscular contraction rippled unseen from neck to ankles. They spoke to each other in the fluting notes of Dolphinese, their mother tongue, for none of them had learned to speak the language of men until they were adults. Having expended some of their pent-up vitality they began to hunt, nibbling a tasty morsel here and a prawn there. Although they all enjoyed the variety of food available in the upper-air world they would from time to time crave their normal diet. After several hours of enjoyment in their own world they would lazily return to the ship and mount the rope ladder trailing from her stern, feeling refreshed and renewed.

Oswald Raynor sat on deck and surveyed the empty ocean which stretched in every direction as far as the eye could see. Triton's domain, he thought, was larger than man's, for the sea covered three-quarters of the earth's surface. Raynor would wait on deck until his friend returned, however long that might be, and as he stood watching the waves for that magic moment when the body of Triton would appear cleaving through the water he thought back to his first sight of him. He remembered he had been holidaying on the research ship with his friend Dr. Crane when suddenly a hundred miles from land a school of dolphins surfaced and vanished again. That was nothing unusual but sitting astride one of them and riding it like a horse with obvious enjoyment and abandon sat a laughing golden-haired boy. Raynor sighed nostalgically and lit another cigar.

It was fine weather as they crossed the Bay of Biscay. They rounded Brest and passing the Channel Islands entered the English Channel and made for the Strait of Dover. A London sea pilot came out from Folkestone and assisted them to Gravesend where the river pilot came aboard and took over. They anchored close to the South Shore, just below Gravesend while arrangements to book a suitable berth were put in motion through the harbor master. Both girls were excited and watched the river traffic with keen interest. They kept close to Triton and asked innumerable questions, which aroused the pilot's interest.

While waiting instructions on where to proceed they were boarded by the water-guard officers of the Customs, and the port health authority officials.

In due course they were notified to proceed to Quebec Dock and started upriver. They followed its curve, passing Tilbury Docks into Galleons Reach, and as they traversed Woolwich Reach passed the Royal Victoria and Albert and King George V Docks on their starboard side. Syn and Vinca leaned over the rail gazing at the busy river in silence. They had never seen anything like this before and they were too fascinated even to chatter. They slowly passed Bugsby's Reach following the sinuous twist of the river as it curved left and entered the Blackwell Reach passing the West India Docks.

They passed Millwall Docks, slowed as they entered Limehouse Reach, edged their way into Greenland Entrance Lock, and entered Greenland Dock. The swing bridge was open and moving very slowly as they entered Canada dock which opened directly into Quebec Dock. The pilot skillfully eased their lovely ship into her berth alongside the dock which completed his task.

Triton shook hands and thanked him and the pilot looked at him curiously, wondering who he was.

"You don't often see a ship like this, and I see she's newly built," he added.

Triton smiled for there was obvious admiration in

his voice. The Pilot turned to go, hesitated and half turned back.

"This is where the old sailing ships used to discharge timber so she'll feel at home here, sir," he said and continued on his way.

Triton's Silver Cloud was waiting for them on the dockside and they climbed in while Nero and Hercules packed the trunk with their personal luggage. Triton insisted that Oswald sit in front and slowly the big car eased its way forward. It passed through the dock gates, entered the main road and swept majestically forward on its way to London. The girls sat in silent astonishment most of the way, fascinated by what they saw.

chapter three

THE CAR STOPPED outside Raynor's house in Eaton Square and the chauffeur, helped by one of the indoor staff, moved in the luggage. The remainder would be brought from the ship later. Triton, or Sir John Averill as he would now be called again, had decided to make London the first stop on their voyage. It would be here rather than in New York, as he had originally intended, that Syn and Vinca would receive their first taste of civilization. They were shown to their rooms wide-eyed and silent after their first ride through a city of men. They had received so many new impressions at once they could hardly sort them out. The dense traffic which appeared to move so fast and the street after street of massed buildings astounded them. Every moment they had expected it to come to an end but it appeared to continue forever. The red buses crammed with people towered over the car and appeared enormous. The girls had window seats and their curious wondering faces almost pushed against the glass in eagerness as they stared out at the bewildering scene.

The crowds in the street and the dense streams of people pouring in and out of the subways reminded them of the vast herring shoals on which they sometimes fed.

"Now we know what a city means," said Vinca.

Syn wrinkled her pretty nose.

"What ghastly smells," she muttered.

"I asked John, you know we must call him that now"—Syn nodded her golden head—"and he said it was gasoline and diesel fumes."

"What's that?"

"I didn't have a chance to ask before we arrived and had to climb out."

Syn looked disappointedly out of the window.

"There's hardly room to walk out there."

"We can always go in a little land ship."

"Car, my dear," said Syn in a slightly superior voice.

"Automobile, darling," replied Vinca.

Both girls looked at each other and burst out laughing.

Oswald Raynor, feeling fatigued, had excused himself and retired to his room. Vicky and John Averill were sitting in the lounge where the duchess was relaxing with a drink and a cigarette. She looked at John and wondered, not for the first time, how old he was. He looked about twenty-five but she remembered reading about his exploit with the great sperm whale while she was still at school and that was sometime ago. It would be easy enough to find out she thought.

"Are you going to stay here, John?"

"Raynor insists and I'm delighted. It's a big house and well staffed for these days." He smiled

27

tolerantly. "The girls will love it. Oswald is quite a gourmet, you know."

"I'm sure they will. They're the most enthusiastic creatures I've ever met and enjoy everything to the full. I've become very fond of them."

"I'm glad to hear it, Vicky."

She looked at him speculatively. "You know Oswald has asked me to stay?"

John nodded.

"My flat is so near I'd rather be at home. Do you want me to continue the girls' education?"

"Please, Vicky, I'm socially uneducated."

She laughed. "You have a natural grace," she said warmly.

He sat relaxed, looking out into the Square. She had never met anyone, she thought, who could remain so still and peaceful. He could explode into astonishing physical action as she well knew but when he sat down there was no fidgeting or restless movements. The sun glinted on his golden hair and the bronze aquiline face was immobile. He is like a statue of Apollo she thought, and brushed such fanciful thoughts aside.

"Both girls are of marriageable age," she said gravely. "Do you wish them to meet eligible young men?"

There was silence and she thought his face clouded. He is fearful of losing them she thought with a pang of jealousy. He was not conscious of such a feeling even if it existed in a deeper level of his mind. If they were like himself, as he knew they were, they had more than a need of the deep sea. It was in their blood as the salts of the sea, he understood, were in the blood of all humans. With them,

28

however, it would be a craving to return regularly to their natural habitat and he wondered how successful a marriage to a human could be under such circumstances. His mind switched to their potential immortality which he had not yet explained to them. He had only to look at himself in a mirror to know that Dr. Crane's assumption that he was immortal except for disease or accident was true. He only spent three months out of every year on the land and then returned to the sea. He could hardly visualize a happy marriage under such conditions.

If the girls returned to a normal earth life they might well forfeit this gift of the sea. They must have their chance of love and happiness however. He would explain things to them and then the choice would be theirs. All these thoughts flitted quickly through his mind before he answered. He turned his quiet gaze on Vicky.

"That's very kind of you. I'd like them to meet as many suitable young men as possible."

The duchess nodded.

"Leave it to me," she said with inward satisfaction.

"I wish them to see all the sights of London and to taste all the pleasures of this great city." He wanted them to understand fully what the world of men could offer. "Will you help me do that, Vicky?"

"Of course, John, and I'll enjoy every minute of it."

"We'll take them out to dinner and introduce them to the theater, the movies and opera. Shopping, beauty parlors and dressmakers will be your responsibility. I'll open an account for them and you can

29

have the pleasure of explaining what a checkbook means."

Vicky made a grimace and John laughed.

"It'll be very interesting to see their reactions to these novel experiences," he said, and Vicky fully agreed with him.

John's chauffeur-driven Rolls was at their disposal all day and every morning after breakfast would fetch the duchess to Eaton Square. Vicky made appointments with her hairdresser in Bond Street which she put high on her list of priorities.

John solemnly handed each girl a checkbook in a neat leather case with a slender gold pen attached to it by a chain. John had taught them while on the island how to read and write and they had received daily lessons from their tutor ever since. Vicky had been busy teaching them deportment and the social graces. They could therefore meet people on an apparently even footing and it was only during a prolonged conversation that their extensive educational gaps might be exposed.

"What is it?" asked Vinca curiously turning it over in her hand.

Vicky took a deep breath, but Syn answered.

"Lloyds Bank something, thirty churkuhs," she read slowly.

"Pronounced checks," added Vicky.

"Why?"

"We'll go into that later," said Vicky hastily.

"When you buy something in a store you have to pay money, you know that."

"Yes," said both girls nodding their heads.

"Instead of carrying money about, you can write the amount on one of these pieces of paper and give it to the store owner. He will then take it to the bank where it will be exchanged for cash."

"Cash?" queried Syn.

"It's another word for money," said Vicky.

"A very satisfactory arrangement," said Vinca blandly, putting the checkbook into her handbag and snapping it shut. Vicky choked while John laughed outright. The girls approached John and looked at him intently.

"It will be your money?" queried Syn.

John nodded.

"Have you enough?" asked Vinca.

"You can spend what you like," he said.

They kissed him lightly, a human custom of which they both approved, and turned to Vicky, eager to go.

Under the careful hands of the duchess they soon blossomed out into stylishly dressed sophisticated young ladies. Their hair styles were distinctive and they spent days being fitted with clothes, for their present wardrobes, though extensive, were ready-made. They emerged as startling beauties and regular manicures and hair sets kept them so. They were always perfectly groomed—their clothes came from the best fashion houses and with their peculiar grace of movement they attracted the eye of every male in their vicinity. The duchess knew she would have no difficulty in finding them willing husbands which she intended to do as soon as possible. From then on she started introducing them to eligible bachelors whenever the opportunity offered.

They fascinated every male who met them, both young and old, and soon each had a bevy of admirers. They frankly loved the adulation and compliments and decided that upper-air men were charming and possessed very good taste. They discussed their admirers' qualities and courting techniques with a frankness that would have shocked the duchess if she had heard them.

Vicky thought it prudent to give them a little homily on men in general about whom there was little she did not know. She did so one evening when the three of them were alone.

Oswald Raynor had been admitted to the London Clinic for observation and Triton was visiting him.

"How are you getting on with your boy friends?" she asked.

"Very well," said Vinca with a satisfied smile.

"They are most charming and attentive," added Syn.

"And are always sending us flowers."

"Or chocolates," said Syn, looking round for a box. She produced a large ornate one from Harrod's and passed it round. The duchess chose one carefully and sighed.

"Men are all the same," she said.

The girls listened silently.

"One of the great differences between men and women is their attitude toward sex. Speaking generally men can enjoy sex without love while a woman can only fully enjoy it with love."

She paused and looked at the two wide-eyed girls.

"I suppose you know all about sex and reproduction?" she asked anxiously and was reassured by their vigorous assent—of course they knew all about it—had they not lived among the dolphins and watched them every year as they courted, made love and gave birth to their babies?

"One has to remember in their favor," continued the duchess, "that men have to take the initiative in lovemaking and in order to be able to take the first steps, they have been given a greater initial sex drive."

Both girls were listening with great interest.

The duchess continued carefully.

"It is necessary for us, therefore, to be able to control their ardor which otherwise could carry them farther than they might intend."

She was putting this over very well she thought.

"Why would you want to do that?" asked Vinca curiously. Vicky raised her eyebrows.

"Do what?"

"Control their ardor," said Syn.

For a moment Vicky was nonplused.

"That is the only way to reproduce," said Vinca firmly.

The duchess swallowed.

"But only after you are safely married," she said.

"You mean for the season until we have our baby," replied Vinca.

The duchess paled.

"What do you mean for the season," she almost squeaked; "marriage is for life."

Both girls looked at each other in surprise and there was an uncomfortable silence.

"Dolphins mate afresh each year and the males play no part in bringing up the young. The child belongs entirely to the mother who rears it devotedly to adulthood." Syn spoke slowly.

"Do you mean, Vicky, that humans only have one mate during their life?"

"Yes, which is why you have to be as certain as you can before you marry."

"Certain of what?"

"That you love each other," replied Vicky.

Vinca looked curiously at the duchess. "You remember introducing me to Mr. Leamont?"

Vicky nodded.

"He distinctly told me that Lydia was his third wife and that after seeing me he thought it was time he had another change."

Trust that old fool Leamont to say the wrong thing if it was humanly possible, thought Vicky.

"It's true that some humans break the accepted custom and divorce their wives to remarry."

"What is this marriage business?" asked Syn.

Vicky sighed and tried to explain. They were fascinated with the concept of love and were prepared to talk about it forever but marriage was different and they were shaken at the idea of publicly pledging themselves for life to one man.

"Let us cut out the idea of any seasonal business," said Vicky shakily. "Remember you are human beings."

"But we may choose the wrong man," wailed Syn.

"That is a risk we all run," said the duchess.

"But is that any reason why we should run it as well?" asked Vinca solemnly.

Vicky took a deep breath.

"There are many good reasons, Vinca," said the duchess firmly. "For instance everyone will consider you bad women if you have children outside marriage, and no nice person will wish to speak to you."

The girls looked startled.

"Would that apply to you?" asked Syn.

The duchess looked at them silently for a moment and then spoke emphatically.

"If you behaved like that I would no longer consider you my friends."

Both Syn and Vinca were appalled yet there were inconsistencies here they could not understand.

"What about Mr. Leamont—you speak to him," said Vinca.

"He's not a friend, like you are."

"But you speak to him," insisted Vinca.

Vicky was wondering how to answer when to her great relief John walked in and she repeated the conversation to him in detail.

He looked at his watch and spoke to the girls in high fluting notes. Vicky guessed it was Dolphinese though she had never heard it before.

Vinca and Syn listened attentively.

When he had finished they rose, kissed him and retired to their rooms without speaking.

"I'm afraid Oswald's rather ill."

"I'm sorry, John, what is it?"

"Hodgkin's disease."

"Is that serious?"

"The doctors say it is, Vicky." He sighed and turned to the bookshelves.

He was very fond of Oswald who had been one of his first human friends and the news had depressed him.

The duchess waited impatiently as long as she could.

"Vinca and Syn are going to be a great problem where the other sex is concerned."

"Do you think so?" he murmured.

Vicky gasped.

"I explained to you their fantastic ideas."

"They are based as you would expect on dolphin behavior whose morality, as far as my observations go, is equal to, if not superior to that of *Homo sapiens*."

Vicky was dying to know what he had said to the girls and the wretch was putting her in the position of having to ask him outright.

"How are you going to deal with it, John?"

"We must give them time to absorb and comprehend the human domestic pattern."

The duchess stamped her foot with frustration.

"What did you say to them just now?" she demanded.

John raised his eyebrows at her vehemence.

"Only that they were to inform me when they found a satisfactory male, before taking any action."

With this the duchess had to be content.

Vinca and Syn would not be separated and they shared a large double room. John visited them on his way to bed. They were both reading and looked up with welcoming smiles as he entered. Vinca patted the side of her bed and he sat down facing them. Syn laid aside her book and looked at him inquiringly.

"Vicky seemed a little upset," observed Vinca.

"I've noticed this reaction in humans when they meet a different code of morality," answered John.

"What's that mean?" asked Syn.

"I've come to speak about something else."

Both girls gave him their full attention.

"Although we are all three humans we are different from any others. Our home is the sea. It's a ruthless environment but it apparently bestows a gift on those of its creatures who can avoid death by violence or disease."

He paused in thought.

"What sort of gift?" they asked eagerly.

"Immortality," he said quietly.

Both gazed at him wide-eyed. Both were familiar with death as part of the unforgiving nature of their background, but neither had given any thought to lifespan. This was a new thought.

"How long do earth people live?" asked Syn.

"Sixty to eighty years."

"How old is Mr. Raynor?"

"About seventy-five I think."

"Do all humans end up like that."

John nodded.

They shivered daintily.

"How terrible," said Vinca.

"Will that happen to us?" asked Syn in horror.

"I don't think it will."

They sighed with relief.

"There are certain problems," he said hesitantly.

"Such as what?" prompted Syn.

"I don't know what would happen if we left the sea forever."

"We could never do that," they exclaimed indignantly.

"But what will you do when you fall in love and marry?" he asked.

They were silent for a while.

"Is it true you marry and live with one man all your life?" asked Vinca.

John nodded his head solemnly.

"That's what Vicky said," interposed Syn. "I

should think it would be better not to get married at all."

"Suppose we make a mistake," said Vinca putting her hand over Triton's.

"You must make certain you don't, my dear."

She pursed her lips doubtfully as he rose and bade them good night. He had wanted them to understand their unique position and to be able to give it some thought before they formed any strong attachments. When they understood themselves better they could do as they wished. Meanwhile there would be a lot of questioning and evaluating.

chapter four

THE DINING ROOM at Eaton Square was large and furnished in heavy, old-fashioned oak. A thick Turkey carpet covered the floor and surrounding the refectory table were high-backed cane chairs. There was always a wide choice of food and John helped himself to bacon and tomatoes from among the silver dishes on the hot plate. A maid brought him in some fresh toast and he was eating and looking at the *Telegraph* when he was joined by Vinca and Syn. They went eagerly to the sideboard and there was a clatter of lids and a muttered discussion before they came to the table.

John looked curiously at their piled plates.

"You'll both get fat."

"We can always swim it off," said Syn airily.

Vinca was too busy eating to answer.

"Any plans for today?"

"We don't know until Vicky comes."

"I want to go underneath again," said Vinca.

John smiled.

"Where's that?" he asked.

"She means where the stairs move up and down and the trains go through holes."

"The subway," said John dryly. "I'm taking you out to the theater tonight," he added.

Vinca swallowed hastily.

"What's a theater?" she asked.

"It is a place where people act," he raised his hand—"I'll explain what acting is in a minute."

They remained expectantly silent while he finished his last mouthful of toast and emptied his cup.

"It takes place in a large building where there is a stage."

"What's a stage?" asked Syn.

John sighed. "You know what a story is?"

They nodded their pretty heads and went on eating as if they were starved.

"Real people take the part of the characters and you see them behaving as they do in the story."

Both girls considered this in silence as they continued with their breakfast.

"That would take hours and hours," said Vinca.

"Will we be there all night?" added Syn.

"I'm saying no more, you must wait and see," he answered. They rode on the subway, lunched at Harrod's, visited the hairdressers and returned to Eaton Square for an early dinner. The car dropped them at the theater and they were shown to their seats. John had considered it prudent to take a box where they would be on their own.

"What a nice little room," said Vinca glancing around before taking a seat. The theater was nearly full and there was the expectancy engendered by a full house just before the curtain rises. The girls leaned forward on the red plush edge of their box,

40

gazed into the auditorium and sensed the feeling of anticipation. Syn looked at John, pointed at the curtains and spoke in a whisper.

"What's behind there?"

"The stage."

Further conversation was stopped by the curtain rising. The play was a modern thriller and very well done. It was a totally new experience for the girls who had no concept of make-believe. Nor was there anything in their own world with which to compare or measure it. The result was complete identification. As soon as the action began their true environment vanished and they were in the sitting room on the stage. Like children at a pantomine everything at the moment was real and they sat forward in their seats enthralled.

A married couple lived in a basement flat and the young wife was blind. They watched fascinated as John the husband left for work and the girl cleared the breakfast table. When she went into the next room a man stealthily entered and began to search. When the young wife reentered he remained perfectly still but she sensed his presence.

"Who is it?" she asked but there was no answer.

"I know someone is there, is it you, John?"

Still silence and Vinca and Syn sat tense gripping the edge of their box.

The girl's voice rose hysterically.

"Don't play games with me, please."

The audience could feel the fear rising in the blind girl. Vinca felt her heart pounding, for the man had a knife in his hand.

"He's standing by the refrigerator," shrieked Vinca involuntarily.

41

"It's not John," shouted Syn.

Heads turned curiously to their box.

"Shut up," hissed Vicky turning scarlet.

The girls suddenly looked contrite and covered their mouths with their hands in dismay.

"Remember it's only make-believe," said John.

Vinca nodded her head, her eyes glued to the stage.

It said a lot for the actors that they took the interruption in their stride and only the man glanced momentarily toward their box. The play developed and the action became more tense until it was again too much for Vinca who shouted out advice to the blind girl.

Some people in the audience hissed for silence and Vicky pulled her own chair to the back of the box. She had never felt more embarrassed in all her life.

The manager had been notified of the disturbance and at the fall of the curtain he knocked on the door and entered quite prepared to ask the occupants to leave.

He was nonplused to see the Duchess of Beaux whom he knew. The rather pink duchess smiled at him.

"Good evening Mr. Beaumont, allow me to introduce you to Miss Vinca Phelan—Miss Sinclaire Phelan, and Sir John Averill."

Mr. Beaumont acknowledged the introduction, a little overcome with the unexpected charm and beauty of the two young ladies and his misjudgment of the situation. He had expected something quite different.

"This is the first play they've seen," said the

duchess confidentially, "and it's so gripping that once or twice they've forgotten it's not real."

Mr. Beaumont felt vaguely complimented and looking into the auditorium realized everyone was gazing at them curiously, some with smiles while others looked and whispered. Neither girl was in the least perturbed though the same could not be said of Vicky.

"We'll persuade them not to take it so seriously in the next act," said John.

"Quite so," murmured Mr. Beaumont rather at a loss.

"What exactly happened?" he asked.

"I warned her where that wicked man was standing," said Vinca unabashed.

Mr. Beaumont looked at her unbelievingly. She was a lovely creature and exquisitely dressed.

"Because you thought it was real?" he asked.

"It seemed like it at the time," said Syn.

Mr. Beaumont smiled and suddenly had a bright idea.

"Would you like to meet the actors?"

"It might prevent a repetition," said Vicky quickly.

"Come with me then." He led the way importantly down a corridor, through a door marked private, and then downstairs to the actors' dressing rooms. He knocked on one of the doors and a cheery voice asked him in. The blind girl was reclining in a chair smoking a cigarette while the villain was half sitting on her dressing table drinking a glass of beer. Vinca was momentarily scandalized while Syn, meeting the gaze of the girl, spoke involuntarily.

"You're not blind then?"

"I hope not, dear," she said smiling.

Mr. Beaumont introduced everyone and there was considerable chatter and laughter.

"We were talking about you just before you came in and wishing we could make as strong an impression on everyone," said the villain to Vinca in undisguised admiration.

Vinca found herself in a peculiar mental state as her intellect and emotions battled with each other. She disliked this man whose portrayal of a villain she had fully accepted. The circumstances had now suddenly changed and here he was in a happy atmosphere obviously on friendly terms with his potential victim. She smiled at him weakly as he came over and spoke to her. Her mind told her he had been playing a part and that he was not necessarily the villain he appeared, but she could not fully discard her emotional reaction.

"Do you like the theater?" he asked looking at her curiously. He wondered who she was as he appraised her beauty.

"I love it."

"What made you call out like that?"

Vinca colored with embarrassment.

"I'm sorry, I hope it didn't spoil things?"

He shook his head, smiling.

"It's the first time I've been to a theater and it all seemed so real. I thought you were going to hurt her," she said accusingly with a straight look from her blue eyes. Further conversation was cut short by the first bell and a charmed Mr. Beaumont showed them the stage on the way back. He was gratified at Vinca and Syn's reaction when they saw the back of the set, the catwalk, spotlights and behind-the-scene workers involved in the production.

They watched the rest of the play spellbound—but in silence, to Vicky's great relief.

The girls could not stop talking about it afterward until at last Vicky was bored to death.

"Can we see it again?" asked Vinca. Relenting, Vicky laughed.

"I wouldn't do that. There're plenty of other plays."

"Are there really?" asked Syn.

"Let's see them all," said Vinca eagerly.

"We can, but only on one condition."

They looked at her questioningly.

"No interruptions—it was very embarrassing."

"We're so sorry, Vicky."

They were both contrite and promised never to do such a thing again.

"It took us by surprise," murmured Syn.

"We interrupted before we realized it," added Vinca apologetically. Vicky laughed at their woebegone expressions.

"There's no harm done," she said to their relief.

Both girls were keen to own a car and began to take daily driving lessons. Vinca was full of enthusiasm and the young man who taught her was delighted with his charming pupil until she sat behind the wheel, when his dominant emotion became one of acute anxiety. Syn, who was the more cautious of the two, learned quickly. Vinca had no idea of machinery and tended to drive as if the car could think for itself. If she had not fascinated the instructor he would have refused to continue the lessons. He took his seat each time full of foreboding and would only use a car with dual controls. Vinca would happily slap in the gears and accelerate and time after time he had to take over control to avoid a collision. Vinca eventually learned to drive and became less of a menace but was furious when Syn passed her test first. She had to take it three times but was jubilant when she passed. In a state of euphoria she went with Vicky to choose a car in one of the smarter showrooms where a salesman explained the advantage of each immaculate machine without even mentioning anything so plebeian as the price. Vinca sat in them all and was more interested in the gadgets than anything else, a fact the salesman was quick to notice. He put her in a lovely Bentley and sold it on the strength of its electric windows.

"I'll have this one," she said when she realized the windows opened and shut by pushing a button.

There were two in the showroom, one black and the other a dark blue.

"Which color would madam like?"

Vinca considered carefully. Vicky was reminded of the concentrated attention Vinca devoted to the purchase of clothes.

"I think I'll have the blue."

"Yes, madam," said the pleased salesman. "Where would madam like it delivered?"

"I'll drive it away now."

"You can't do that, madam. It has to be licensed and insured. But you can have it in two days."

"If I can't take it now I won't have it," said Vinca firmly. This ultimatum produced a flurry of activity. Her bank was telephoned, and papers filled in and signed and eventually a triumphant Vinca drove the car out into a side road. It was twenty yards to the main road and nosing out she collided with a car coming from the right.

"Damn," said Vinca.

The duchess sat immobile. She decided this was the first and last time she would go with Vinca to buy a car.

The driver of the other car descended in a cloud of outrage, quickly dispersed by Vinca's charm. The combination of beauty and Bentley was too much and he only just saved himself from apologizing.

The necessary formalities over, Vinca backed the car twenty yards and got out.

"I won't be a minute, Vicky," she said and disappeared into the showroom leaving the duchess sitting rigidly in the front seat.

The salesman hurried over to her.

"I'll have the black one," she said calmly.

The salesman's training enabled him to remain impassive although this girl bought Bentleys like tea cakes.

"Certainly, madam; where shall we deliver it?"

"I'll take it now."

The young man swallowed.

"But what about the other one madam?"

"Some idiot has run into it."

"The new Bentley," he squeaked.

Vinca looked at him curiously.

"I don't want a damaged car so I'll have the other."

"Of course, madam."

There was more paper signing and arranging and Vinca became the owner of the black Bentley. The Duchess of Beaux insisted on driving it home or going by taxi, much to Vinca's annoyance. Vinca liked the car, which was a dream to drive, but, like Triton, exhibited little personal pride of possession. Her upbringing was such that ownership was still almost an alien concept. No one ever owned anything in the sea. If her car was lost or stolen she would either buy another or do without and there would be no emotional repercussions except perhaps one of annoyance. This was something the Duchess of Beaux with all her experience did not grasp, and Vinca's behavior appeared to her feckless and extravagant. In reality it was neither. She had no innate sense of money value and could not be expected to have one. Such a sense can only be achieved by experience and even then many people never acquire it. Triton had told her to spend what she liked and she accepted the statement literally—as he knew she would.

The duchess was pleased to get home. Vinca and Syn were charming girls but could be very wearing at times. You never knew what they would do next she thought as she sank into a hot bath. She was relaxing with a cigarette when the telephone rang. She lifted the receiver.

"Vicky, you're holding out on me," said a pleasant masculine voice.

"Is that you, James?"

"Who else, my dear."

"What do you mean, holding out on you?"

"I've just seen you with a delectable creature in a new Bentley, who is she?"

"What color was the car?" asked the duchess.

There was a pause of surprise at the other end of the line.

48

"That's a funny question, Vicky."

"Well!"

"It was black."

The duchess smiled. He hadn't seen the debacle then—for which she was grateful. She had felt like a puppet on show sitting in the front seat with everyone staring at her. She had not felt so acutely uncomfortable since the incident in the theater.

"Who is she?"

"Someone too good for you, James."

"You're cutting me to the quick and adding pain to my curiosity."

She took a long pull on her cigarette, and exhaled slowly.

"Are you there, Vicky?"

"I'll take pity on you, James."

"When?"

"Don't be so impatient. She'll be at my next cocktail party. Goodbye, James," she said sweetly and hung up.

Lord James Renshaw was one of the most eligible bachelors in town and it was time he settled down she thought. He was in the Foreign Office and very popular with the ladies. He was an experienced man of the world and if he had set his sights on Vinca she wouldn't stand a chance thought the duchess with satisfaction. His title alone would be very attractive to a young inexperienced girl like Vinca, but in thinking this she showed less than her usual perspicacity.

Vicky was anxious to see both Syn and Vinca married, though she had not yet consciously faced her motivation. It was sufficient reason for the present that Triton had asked her to see that both girls met as many eligible bachelors as possible from whom they could choose husbands if they so wished. Her mind dwelt on Triton as she discarded her cigarette and began to soap her arms. He was an enigma she longed to understand. She was fascinated by his strange ability to live beneath the sea, his handsome aquiline face and the fluid movements of his powerful body. She had made it her business to discover his age and was one of the few people who marveled at his youth. She intended obeying his request literally and would continue to introduce young men until both girls were safely married. She sighed with satisfaction at her decision and began to wash one of her long and elegant legs.

The cocktail party given by the Duchess of Beaux was a great success. Syn and Vinca were the center of attraction and males of all ages hovered round, offering them tidbits to eat and refilling their glasses. The girls thoroughly enjoyed themselves, eagerly sampling the variety of interesting appetizers and sipping their cocktails with relish. Their enthusiastic and wholehearted enjoyment of everything was refreshing, and everyone wondered who they were, and wanted to meet them.

"Here I am, Vicky," said a good-looking young man who suddenly materialized at her elbow.

The party was in full swing. Vicky smiled and taking his elbow eased him with practiced skill through the packed room.

"Vinca, my dear, here's an old friend of mine: Lord James Renshaw—Miss Vinca Phelan."

Renshaw gazed at Vinca and felt the beat of his own pulse. He took her small hand in his and spoke confidently.

"I've been dying for this moment since I first saw you." His voice was pleasant and conveyed a sense of earnestness and Vinca surveyed him with interest.

"Go on," she said.

He gave a boyish smile and explained how he had telephoned Vicky after seeing them both in the car.

"I just had to meet you," he said and did not bother to hide his obvious admiration.

Vinca enjoyed it all and when he asked if she would go to the theater and dine with him, she produced a little diary and wrote down the date.

"What play would you like to see?" he said and she mentioned three.

"Why those?" he asked in surprise.

"I've seen all the others."

"You're obviously keen on the theater."

"I love it," said Vinca frankly.

Syn was receiving the same amount of attention and the observant duchess smiled faintly for at this rate neither girl was likely to remain single for long. She thought of Triton which she did often now.

He neither drank nor smoked and he abhorred cocktail parties. She had excused him from coming only on the understanding that he dine with her afterward. She was giving him a wonderful meal after which they could relax and talk. It was a pity he did not drink alcohol she thought, and a small frown wrinkled her lovely forehead—a good brandy after dinner could do wonders.

Both girls were in the habit of discussing events with Triton at the end of the day. They brought him their problems and discussed the more puzzling aspects of human behavior. If he had retired they would go up to his room and they often talked late into the night, time having no meaning for them. They were accustomed to hunt when they were hungry, race through the sea when the fancy took them, and rest on the sun-drenched sand when they were tired. One of the hardest things they had to learn, during their sojourn in the upper-air world among civilized men, was to govern their actions by the hands of a clock.

Both girls were intrigued by restaurants and the variety of possible dishes astonished them. The exchange of a dirty piece of paper for a magnificent meal struck them as delightfully convenient and in the early days they stuffed themselves disgracefully.

They would sample a new dish in a different restaurant several times a day and eventually realized that even meals had fixed hours, and so were governed by the clock.

This time-control of human life was an alien concept to them which they found difficult to accept or understand. The arbitrary rules of these little machines, which they noticed on people's bodies and in larger forms on public buildings, they found irksome and unpleasant.

They imposed a restriction on their freedom and a curtailment of natural inclination, and for a long time were a source of mild anxiety. This reaction was a reflection of the girls' essential wildness and when they discussed it with Triton he admitted to the same sensations when he first lived among men.

Triton was reading in bed when they came in. Syn relaxed in an easy chair while Vinca draped herself on the bed. They still both felt the restriction of clothes and were wearing diaphanous nighties which they hardly knew they had on. In spite of enjoying themselves to the full they were anxious for knowledge and worked hard at their studies. They were curious and greedy for new sights, smells and tastes and this extended into the field of intellectual effort. They were as inquisitive as imported apes and enjoyed acquiring knowledge as much as experiencing pleasure. Study itself was a pleasure which they enjoyed with gusto. They learned quickly but whether this was really due, as Triton's tutor had once suggested, to their minds remaining fallow until puberty was open to discussion.

Vinca was fascinated by animals, while Syn was equally attracted to machines and they both wanted to study these subjects. Vinca broached the matter first.

"It's zoology you want to read," said Triton.

"Can I?" asked Vinca eagerly.

"Certainly. As you are so interested we'll make it your main subject."

She threw her arms round his neck, kissed him and remained lying at his side. She looked abandoned with her nightie exposing more of her limbs than it covered. These three however had grown up and lived together without a thought for clothes or even any knowledge about them as far as the girls were concerned. The picture they made therefore would have given an observer a very false impression.

"What about you, Syn, is there anything you particularly like?"

She nodded her head vigorously and her golden hair cascaded round her shoulders.

"Machines, Triton. I want to know all about cars and flying machines."

"So you shall, Syn, nothing could be easier."

While maintaining their basic studies they specialized in these two subjects. Syn was taught the secrets of the automobile and in due course the helicopter in which she was primarily interested. She was soon servicing her own car and learning to fly and eventually obtained a pilot's license.

Vinca's first interest was sea life and she was coached by a marine biologist who took her to the best aquariums in the country. She worked hard and accumulated a respectable library on this subject. She was most curious to know how Pussy, their octopus, could so miraculously change his color, how he could flow fast over the sand like a live liquid and ooze through a crack obviously too narrow to admit his body. How did the electric eels work, she wondered, and where was the most vital place to stab a shark. Her pretty head was full of such questions and while other girls of her age would be sprawling on the floor listening to pop music, she sprawled on the floor and read the answers to these mysteries.

chapter five

WHILE VINCA SPENT several afternoons a week visiting aquariums and museums Syn was taught the secrets of the internal-combustion engine. She bought some smart overalls and with a smut on her nose looked enchanting. Her teachers gave her their full attention and she learned quickly, having a natural mechanical aptitude.

She soon began to be puzzled and one day questioned John about her problem.

"Internal-combustion engines always need fuel to make them work don't they?"

"That's correct," admitted John.

She looked perplexed.

"How is it the *Poseidon* carries no fuel then, either for her own engines or the launches?"

"I wondered how long it would be before you asked me that."

She looked at him curiously.

"They are electric motors and work on electricity."

"But there are no batteries," replied Syn.

55

"The *Poseidon* works on a new prinicple which is still an industrial secret. She utilizes power which is broadcast from Scotland."

The full significance of the statement escaped her.

"It's broadcast like sound waves you mean?"

"That's right, but I don't wish anyone to know about it yet."

"That means no more smelly gasoline."

"Exactly," said Triton.

She tried to work out the implication of fuelless machines and realized, even with her insufficient knowledge, that it would produce tremendous changes.

"Can I see the broadcasting machine?"

"Any time you like. Dr. Cunningham, whose baby it is, would be delighted to show you."

The following week she drove to Scotland and stayed a few days with the Cunninghams. She was fascinated with the power plant and the broadcasting machine but could not grasp how it worked. When she returned Vinca sensed a change in her. She regarded her speculatively several times while they were getting ready for bed. There was a faraway look in her eyes which made Vinca curious.

"Tell me about it?" she said softly.

Syn looked startled for a moment and then smiled reminiscently.

"I've met a marvelous young man."

"Have you?" said Vinca breathlessly.

Syn spoke in a dreamy voice and described the virtues and fascinating appearance of Antony Watson.

"He sounds marvelous," breathed Vinca.

"You'll meet him soon."

"When?"

Syn shrugged her pretty shoulders.

"In a few days. He's going to ring me as soon as he returns to London."

She looked at Vinca.

"What about your James Renshaw. He's been very attentive since meeting you."

Vinca nodded her head with satisfaction.

"He's lovely," she said.

"I'm sure he thinks the world of you."

"Do you?" said Vinca eagerly.

Syn nodded her head wisely. "You can see by the way he looks at you."

Vinca's eyes were shining. "I can't wait to meet your Antony," she said.

They talked long into the night like the little girls they really were.

Antony Watson arrived in London late at night. He could not wait to see Syn again and phoned early the following morning. John had noted with some amusement how Syn rushed to the telephone every time it rang and realized something was going on but made no reference to it. Syn would tell him in her own good time if she wished to, and if she did not that was her business.

The three of them were having breakfast when Antony telephoned and Syn returned to the table in excitement.

"It's him," she said to Vinca and turning to John told him all about it. Not long afterward Vinca received a call from James Renshaw and both girls finished their breakfast with smug satisfaction.

John saw very little of them in the days that followed. Both girls were in love and walked in a world of their own. John worked at the office during the day but he missed them in the evening. Their nightly talks became less frequent as they arrived home late from a supper party or nightclub and flopped into bed. They were having the time of their lives and enjoying every minute of it.

Vicky watched events closely and did her best to see that John was not too lonely. She frequently asked him round to supper and made a habit of dropping in to see him at other times. She always spoke about the girls and subtly prepared him for the inevitable break. She realized his deep attachment more than he did, she thought. He had brought them up and shared their companionship in the sea and she sensed his devotion to them. When they married it would be a terrible loss to him, even if he did not seem to realize it. It would make a gap, she now admitted to herself, she was prepared to fill and she did her best to charm and console him.

John needed little sleep and would read in bed often late into the night. He heard the front door slam, and looked at his watch. It was only midnight, quite early for his little night birds he thought. After bathing they paid him a visit and made themselves comfortable on his bed.

"How are you enjoying life in the city of men?"

"It's marvelous," said Vinca.

"Superb," added Syn.

"Oswald will be coming home soon."

"How is he?" asked Syn.

"Not very well I fear."

The girls looked at each other.

"When he gets back he'll need rest and quiet and I don't think we should stay here," said Triton.

"Could we have an apartment on our own when we move?" asked Vinca.

John looked surprised.

"There's no reason why you shouldn't," he said after a pause.

"We don't want to leave you but we would like a private place to entertain our friends," explained Syn.

"Humans aren't like dolphins and won't court in public you know," said Vinca artlessly.

"So I believe," said John dryly.

"Are you courting seriously?" he added.

They nodded their pretty heads solemnly and he listened to the virtues of James Renshaw and Antony Watson until for the first time in their relationship he was bored.

He held up his hand and stopped the spate of eulogies.

"I'm sure they're wonderful and I'd like to meet them. You'd better not tell me any more until I do."

They both looked so disappointed that he relented and by the time they went to bed he wondered how the two young men could bear to live among ordinary mortals.

"I'll rent an apartment for you," he said as they were leaving.

They hesitated.

"That's what you want, isn't it?"

"What about you?" they asked.

"I'll probably stay here, Oswald would like it. If I get bored I can always take Vicky out."

They both wanted their own quarters but they suddenly realized it would mean parting from John and they felt a sense of insecurity. His reference to

Vicky produced a resistance they did not understand. Living on their own suddenly did not seem quite such a good idea.

"Can we have an apartment near you?"

"It's difficult to get one at all, but I'll do the best I can."

They thanked him and departed quietly, without their ususal exuberance.

John found a pleasant furnished apartment overlooking Hyde Park and helped the girls move in. They were both quiet as they packed. Their luggage was delivered and the three of them drove over in the Rolls. They looked rather miserable when he was ready to go and clung to him when they kissed him goodbye.

"I'm not leaving the country," he said smiling.

They laughed, but their laughter was near to tears.

John handed each of them a small package before leaving. They were like excited little girls when they received presents.

"What is it?" they asked eagerly as they began to undo them.

"Don't open them now," said John and they looked at him questioningly.

"They are magic presents and you must not see them until twelve o'clock tonight."

As they unpacked and put away their clothes they glanced frequently at the mysterious parcels.

"What do you think they are?" asked Vinca.

Syn slipped a silk frock over a hanger.

"It could be jewelry from the size."

"But he said they were magic."

"I don't know what he means by that," replied Syn.

Vinca picked up hers and shook it gently near her shell-like ear but it remained silent and mysterious.

"What a ghastly long time to wait," she wailed.

The evening arrived at last but at eleven o'clock, time seemed to stop.

Vinca kept looking at her watch, the hands of which seemed hardly to move. She listened to it repeatedly, amazed each time to hear it ticking.

"Let's get ready for bed," said Syn.

At five minutes to twelve they lay side by side, their presents in their hands and exactly at twelve they began excitedly to undo them.

They made exclamations of delight as each unwrapped a beautiful pair of earrings with rings to match. The earrings were miniature gemmed wings which swept backward over their ears. They leaped out of bed and put them on before the mirror; and then slipped on the rings.

"Aren't they lovely?" said Vinca.

Syn turned her head to and fro gazing at her reflection critically and thought how well they suited her.

"What did he mean by saying they were magic," she murmured.

Both girls suddenly froze as they heard a small voice whisper in their ear.

"Don't you think they are?"

Incorporated in the earrings was a miniaturized receiver while hidden in the ring was a minute transmitter both of which derived their power from the air.

Syn and Vinca looked round the room and then at each other.

"Where are you?" they squealed in excitement.

They heard John's miniature laugh.

"Speak into the ring."

Both girls began to talk at once.

"One at a time or I can't hear you."

"Where are you?" asked Syn in amazement.

"In bed at Eaton Square."

"Can you hear me?" said Vinca breathlessly.

"Of course I can."

John was delighted with the success of this new toy. He was in fact much addicted to gadgetry but often used the girls as an excuse to indulge himself. His home, and indeed even the *Poseidon* abounded with devices he had had installed supposedly to astonish and delight his wards. Now he chuckled and spoke in fluting Dolphinese.

Syn and Vinca jumped into bed and the three of them "talked" long into the night.

Both girls were enchanted with their presents. It enabled them to keep close to John while enjoying their freedom and independence. They were both self-contained and physically fearless or they would never have survived the ruthless environment of their childhood. No one who met them during their life upon the land ever fully realized their origin and how near they were to the wild. Even the Duchess of Beaux, who knew their complete history, could not appreciate how they felt in the alien environment of civilization. The manners and behavior patterns she had taught them and which they had picked up with such facile speed fooled her. They slipped unconsciously into the category of nice young girls and

their unique origin was forgotten. With all her experience the duchess was unable to put herself in their
shoes. They had suddenly been transplanted from
one world to another. The quiet sea-green world
beneath the waves which was their natural home and
where they had always lived had suddenly been
exchanged for the raucous, smoky industrialized
world of men. The dangers of their own world they
knew well but this strange environment made them
feel subconsciously uneasy. It was a world they
knew nothing about and the only person they knew
they could trust was Triton, as they thought of him,
in spite of using his earthly name of John which
sounded strange on their tongue. His gifts to them
were therefore priceless for they were tantamount to
having him always at their side. John knew well how
they felt, for he had been through the same experience himself. They would still be together, he
thought, not realizing he was at the same time as-
suaging his own loneliness.

Lord Renshaw lived quietly at the Albany. He
had received the best this world could offer in birth,
brains and wealth. He was an educated, cultured
cosmopolitan and aware of most of the follies and
weaknesses of human nature. He had known many
women but none like Vinca. Her slender beauty,
dark hair and peculiar physical grace delighted him.
The direct and eager gaze of her blue eyes and her
ingenuous enthusiasm captivated him.

But with all his experience he failed to understand
her, which, considering he knew nothing of her history, might not be entirely his fault.

If he had been aware of her unique origin he

might not have made the mistakes he did. Reasons and assumptions that would have been valid for earthly girls did not apply in the same way to Vinca. James Renshaw continued to pay devoted attention to her, unaware of all this.

Vinca found James a delightful, witty and knowledgeable companion. When he realized her keen appreciation of taste and smell he took her to the most exclusive restaurants where the food and wines were chosen for gourmets. In a quiet, almost reverent atmosphere they would eat an exquisite meal and drink rare vintages. Vinca loved these evenings, as well as all the others. They went to theaters, night clubs and the movies, and out of curiosity he took her to a midnight service at St. Paul's. She enjoyed each new experience indiscriminately and imagined herself in love with James, a very easy thing for a young girl to do.

After the theater he had taken her to a nightclub. Dancing with Vinca had amazed him. She was gossamer light in his arms and followed his every movement with effortless grace. If he shut his eyes he could have been dancing with himself, except for one small hand on his shoulder and the other in his. They danced a lot for Vinca enjoyed this as much as she did everything else. Both she and Syn had taken to dancing very quickly and their delighted instructor had suggested they take it up seriously.

In the middle of a dance Vinca stopped.

"Damn," she said.

She stepped daintily out of her panties and tucked the wisp of material in her handbag.

"The wretched elastic broke," she said looking at

him with a smile and then continued imperturbably to dance.

Her dress was a silken sheath and James Renshaw was very much aware of her body as they continued. Vinca forgot the incident but her partner could not, and he wondered if this delightful creature was more experienced than he had thought. He would have expected some slight confusion under such circumstances but there had been none. He would have been even more confused had he known that her reaction would have been just the same had she lost all her clothes instead of just her panties. Nakedness was a natural state to Vinca and could never shame or embarrass her.

At the end of the evening he suggested she return to his apartment for a drink. Vinca was still proud of her own quarters and being anxious to show them off insisted he return with her.

She showed him over the apartment.

"I'll get you coffee and brandy," she said and going into the kitchen put on the percolator. To enter her bedroom she had to go through the living room.

"Have you been here long?" he asked as she passed.

"Only a few weeks."

She sat in front of her mirror and reapplied her lipstick as he stood at the door.

"It's a nice apartment, but not exactly what I expected."

She looked at him in the mirror.

"What did you expect?" she asked curiously.

He hesitated and spoke slowly.

"Something more indicative of your personality."

He strolled in and looked at the pictures.

"For instance every picture appears to be a sea-scape."

Vinca laughed.

"They're the only things that belong to us," she said and became thoughtful. Both she and Syn missed the sea which was beginning to tug and pull at them. They dreamed at night of its cool green depths and longed to return to its arms.

He came up behind her and put his hands on her shoulders.

"What are you thinking of, my dear?"

"The sea," she whispered pulling herself back to the present. He leaned forward and kissed her hair while she watched him with interest in the mirror.

His hands slid down her arms and across her front and he noticed how still she sat without the slight movement of resistance he had half expected. He raised her gently from the seat and turning her round looked into her blue eyes before bending his head and kissing her.

Now she was getting somewhere, thought Vinca, she was about to learn the courting habits of upper-air men.

He led her unresisting to the bed and as he gently pulled down the zipper her frock fell to the floor at her feet leaving her only in a slip and brassiere. He felt the blood begin to pound in his temples as he gently laid her on the bed and kneeled beside her. He was certain now from her behavior that she was experienced in the arts of love and suddenly felt a disappointment. She had seemed to him in some indefinable way different and if he had been told that he was the first person to make love to her he would not now have believed it. His emotions washed away the momentary pang as his hands wandered over her lovely body. Vinca lay there detached and interested. The removal of her clothes partly or completely produced no erotic emotion in her. She could have dined and danced naked and at ease with anybody and it would in fact have felt more natural to her than wearing clothes. He slipped out of his jacket and lay beside her. He was in no hurry and his thoughts were concerned more with his partner than himself, which was perhaps why he was such a success with the opposite sex. He was uninhibited by moral values but an unselfish lover. He kissed her gently first and then more passionately. Vinca ran her hand through his thick black hair and watched him with intense interest. The front door opened and closed and he froze on the bed.

"It's only Syn," murmured Vinca and he relaxed. He started making love to her again when, to his horror, Syn walked in and ignoring them made up her face in the mirror while he lay on the bed in acute embarrassment. She strolled out again unconcernedly and Vinca continued to stroke his hair as if nothing had happened. Having realized the situation she would not come in again, he thought, and relaxed. It was really rather clever the way Syn had handled an awkward situation, he thought, ignoring the whole thing as if she had not seen them. He heard Syn and Antony talking in the next room and making up his mind that both girls were not unused to situations like this he returned to his lovemaking reassured.

Syn made coffee and offered Antony a liqueur which he refused. She loved Antony who was charming and polite and obviously deeply in love with her, but her thoughts kept returning to the bedroom. Vinca was obviously being courted, while Antony had done nothing like that with her. He had kissed her of course but that was all. Her curiosity to know what was going on at last overcame her and with a muttered apology to Antony she returned to the bedroom. She would make up her face and be able to watch in the mirror.

Vinca meanwhile was becoming bored. James was too worked up to realize his partner was not emotionally participating. Such an experience seldom came his way. He never dreamt that Vinca's love for him was entirely idealistic, that she was a little girl in love with love. He might not have continued if he had realized it but he never did. No well-brought-up young girl could have allowed such intimacies so calmly if it was the first time. So James continued quite unaware of the true situation. He was horrified when Syn strolled in again and sitting at the dressing table began to make up her face again leisurely. Lying on the bed in disarray he felt acutely embarrassed. He glanced at Vinca and was shocked to see her quite unconcerned. He lay motionless, feeling a bigger fool every minute, and wondered if the wretched girl would never go. Vinca lay there feeling disappointed. She had not known exactly what to expect but the experience had fallen flat. She realized it had not for James, or at least she thought it had not. Perhaps they were different from upper-air people, and she wondered if her sister might have felt differently. James' embarrassment was slowly turning to anger, and the thought crossed his mind that the two of them might be playing with him. Syn should have known someone was in the bedroom the first time. All the lights in the flat were on, and she most certainly knew the second time.

He glanced again at the delectable creature in his arms, and found her gazing into space, her thoughts obviously elsewhere.

Syn left the room, but all his ardor had gone.

"Are these the usual preliminaries to a seasonal child?" asked Vinca.

He lifted his head and gazed at her almost open-mouthed.

"What?"

"I mean is this the usual courting procedure?"

He flushed with anger at being made to feel an inadequate fool.

"I presume you don't approve," he said sarcastically.

She stroked his face, not wanting to hurt him but he pushed her hand away and rose from the bed.

"I'm sorry," she said contritely, "try it with my sister, she might enjoy it."

"You bitch," he said involuntarily. He felt a deep anger, certain now these two girls were making a fool of him. He would see they did not do that twice.

"I hope I haven't upset you," said Vinca contritely.

He shook his head without speaking.

"What does bitch mean?" she asked in a small voice.

He looked at her lying on the bed, small and helpless, and suddenly felt a brute.

"Don't you really know?"

She shook her head.

"Honest I don't."

He cleared his throat and hesitated. He could of course be mistaken about the whole affair.

"It's a term of endearment," he muttered and left the room. He bade the other two a cursory good night and slammed out of the apartment.

"Whatever's the matter with him?" asked Antony in surprise.

"I can't imagine," said Syn in astonishment.

Syn and Antony were perfectly suited to each other. They were both young and idealistic. Antony regarded Syn as a sort of goddess, an attitude of mind reminiscent of an earlier age. Syn loved Antony without any knowledge of love and tended to treat him as if he were a personal possession. Antony looked after Syn as if she were made of glass and fetched and carried earnestly.

Antony, though only twenty-three, had a degree in chemistry and a promising job with a big industrial group. They discussed marriage and income, and Antony was astonished and shocked at Syn's attitude toward money and her complete lack of interest in it. He was particular to a degree and kept a careful record of his expenses.

"I have some money," she volunteered.

Antony did not know whether to be pleased or not. He would have liked her to be entirely dependent on him.

"How much do you have?" he asked.

Syn hesitated, not quite knowing how to answer.

"I don't know exactly."

"How do you know what to spend then?"

"I just write a check," said Syn sweetly.

Antony was dumfounded.

"You can't do that."

Syn looked surprised.

"You might write a check for more money than you have and there would be trouble."

Syn was not interested in the complexities of finance. Machinery was different and she would spend patient and happy hours mastering the mechanical intricacies of an internal-combustion engine. Financial matters bored her, besides which she was confident that John would have warned her of any risk. She shrugged the subject aside but Antony was not to be put off so easily. He insisted that her financial situation be clarified so they knew where they were. As the account was too recent for her to have received any statement he took her round to the bank. Her guardian had probably put a few hundred pounds into a checking account for her, but it was important she knew enough not to overdraw. It was very wrong of Sir John not to have explained matters more thoroughly to her he thought.

On the way he explained the situation while Syn showed her boredom and gazed at the busy London crowds that never ceased to amaze her.

At his prompting she asked the teller how much stood to her credit and in a short time he returned and gave her a folded slip of paper. Without looking at it she passed it to Antony. He gazed at the amount in petrified astonishment for it was the best part of a hundred thousand pounds.

"Is anything the matter?"

Antony swallowed and shook his head, and slipping the paper in his pocket they left the bank. He was very quiet as they returned to her apartment and Syn looked at him curiously several times. He was

71

withdrawn and thoughtful. What sort of guardian could she have, he wondered, who would put a sum like that in a checking account for her to spend as she liked. Safely invested in gilt-edged stock it would bring in at a minimum five thousand pounds a year or nearly a hundred pounds a week. It was almost indecent to leave such a sum in a checking account. It should be safely invested and he began to explain the situation.

"You can do as you like with it," she said, which embarrassed him.

"I'll discuss it with your guardian when we're engaged," he said.

She turned to him with interest and listened enthralled to this upper-air custom. She was thrilled when she learned it involved the giving and accepting of a ring.

"Let's go now and choose one."

He laughed at her.

"I can't afford an expensive one."

She squeezed his arm.

"The value will lie in its meaning, and that you are giving it to me, darling."

Syn was excited and longing to tell Vinca and John, not to mention Vicky. She seemed to have lost her fear of marriage to one man for life but that was because it was Antony. The idea still shocked her in theory and still appeared dangerous except with him. They would live happily together forever she was certain. Antony wrote an enthusiastic letter to his mother who was at Pelican's Rest, their house in Jamaica. After his father's death she had spent more and more time there. He was full of praise about

Syn, and eulogized on her beauty and charm of character but failed to mention anything about her family or social standing.

Della Lord Watson felt anxious after reading the letter, and wondered if the absence of such vital information held any significance. What sort of girl was Synclaire Phelan she wondered. She folded the letter carefully and decided to return to London immediately and find out.

John was the first to hear the news. Syn burst in on him and threw her arms around his neck.

"Antony and I are engaged, and I'm so happy," she said. He gently unwound her arms and looked into her lovely tear-stained face.

"Why are you crying then?"

She smiled at him and shook her head.

"I don't know, isn't it silly!"

"Humans sometimes do that in moments of joy," he said kindly.

"Look." She displayed her ring proudly.

"It's lovely, Syn. Antony is a very lucky man and I hope he knows it."

"You do like him, don't you."

"Of course I do, you couldn't have picked anyone better."

She squeezed his hand gratefully. "I'm so pleased," she whispered.

Vinca was equally delighted and admired her sister's engagement ring and the added importance she thought it gave her. John was reading at his desk when he felt a tingle in his finger. He twisted his ring palmward and by supporting his head in his left hand brought the ring close to his ear while he continued to study the document in front of him, a report from Dr. Noyes on the progress of the computer. He spoke into the ring on his other hand, as he turned a page of the report.

"Yes."

"Isn't it wonderful news about Syn," said Vinca's small voice.

"Marvelous," he said.

"She says you like him."

"Don't you, Vinca?"

"Of course I do, he's very nice, but do you think he's good enough for Syn?"

John hesitated.

"I don't think anyone is good enough for either of you." There was a little gasp in his ear, and he smiled.

"But I think he's probably as good an upper-air man as you can find."

A delighted little laugh sounded in his ear.

"I'll tell her what you said," said Vinca.

There was silence and he absentmindedly twisted the ring back into postition and continued reading.

Dr. Noyes' work was beginning to bear fruit. He was slowly overcoming the difficulties presented by the electron-lattice computer. This entirely new conception of a computer was at last beginning to take shape and John finished reading the report with satisfaction.

He put it carefully in the safe and thought of Syn. He could see her slender body and long flaxen hair as they sped together through their green and watery world. He remembered the calm comradely glance of her green eyes, and sharply stopped himself reminiscing. What would he do this evening, he wondered.

He felt flat and for once did not enjoy the idea of reading. Suddenly making up his mind he telephoned Vicky. Vicky was an astute woman who now admitted to herself that she was in love with the astonishing Sir John Averill. Since hearing Syn's news she had been sitting by the telephone reading. She knew better than John did himself how Syn's engagement would unsettle him and after letting the phone ring several times she picked it up.

"Is that you, Vicky?"

"Yes, John."

"Are you doing anything this evening?"

She paused before answering.

"There are several things I should do."

"Forget them, Vicky, and have dinner with me."

"It sounds nice," she said reluctantly.

There was a pause.

"What about it, Vicky?"

"Come round and I'll see what I can do," she said and replaced the receiver with a smile.

She went into the dining room and checked the table which was tastefully laid for two. She lit the candles and went into the kitchen. Everything was ready, and slipping a couple of bottles of wine into the refrigerator she went into the bedroom to change.

Vicky, Duchess of Beaux, was a beautiful woman. When she emerged from her bedroom she was ravishing. Her clothes were loose and silky and while covering her almost primly showed every curve and movement of her lovely figure. She entertained John as only a clever and experienced woman could.

The dinner was exquisite and each dish his favorite. Vicky was charming and sympathetic and John sank into a cocoon of mental and physical comfort. Later in the evening he found himself on a deep sofa with a warm and vibrant Vicky in his arms and the small ache deep inside him was forgotten.

chapter six

VINCA HAD NOT HEARD from James Renshaw since his abrupt departure from the apartment and she wondered why. He was the most interesting of all the men she had met so far and she secretly hoped that he would one day offer her a ring such as Syn had received. She felt somehow at a disadvantage without one. When she went out with her sister it gave her the feeling of being incompletely dressed.

They both worked during the day, Vinca at her zoology, and Syn with her beloved machinery. Every evening Syn spent with Antony, leaving Vinca on her own. Although Vinca had many invitations to go out they were mostly from people who did not interest her and she began to spend many of her evenings with John, much to Vicky's annoyance. He was always pleased to see her, and even if he had a date with Vicky thought nothing of bringing her along, a practice which the duchess found intolerable. She wondered what had happened to James Renshaw who she knew had been very interested in Vinca. They must have quarreled over something, she thought with irritation, and she began to think of other eligible bachelors she knew.

John had told her that the girls' birthday was on the twenty-third of the following month and that he wanted to arrange a party for them. It would be the first birthday party they had ever celebrated.

Vicky had been giving some thought to this and to the possible guests. It would be a good excuse to ring up James, for he must certainly be one of the party, and probe the present situation.

She rang him up at the Albany.

"I haven't seen you about lately, James."

"I've been busy, Vicky. How goes it with you?"

"So-so, my dear. You remember the Phelan sisters?"

"Yes."

"One of them has got engaged."

There was a pause at the other end.

"Which one?" asked James.

"Synclaire."

James suddenly had a feeling of relief. He had avoided Vinca because of hurt pride. Although he was annoyed and even angry with her she kept returning to his thoughts. He still could not make up his mind about her but knew now that he must see her again, and suddenly realized he was longing to do so.

"Are you still there, James?"

"Yes."

"I'm ringing you up to tell you that I'm arranging a birthday party for the two girls. It's going to be a really good one and we would all like you to be there."

"I'd love to come. When is it?"

Feeling reassured Vicky told him.

"Damn!"

"What is it."

"I can't come—there's a Foreign Office ball."

"What a shame," murmured the duchess. "I'll have to find someone to replace you."

"Wait a minute, Vicky, do you think they would like to come to the ball?"

She considered carefully. There would be John and herself, Antony and Syn and Vinca and James. It would be better than a party for they would almost certainly pair off and she would have more of John's company.

"It would mean five invitations."

James laughed.

"I'm in charge of the list, so that's no trouble."

"I'll ask Sir John and let you know," said Vicky.

When Vicky told John he thought it was a good idea. It would be a new experience which he thought both girls would enjoy.

"It will be a good setting for my birthday present."

"What would that be?" asked Vicky curiously.

But John laughed and would not tell her.

James Renshaw's mind was full of Vinca while he waited to hear from the duchess. What a lovely, delightful creature she was! He longed to hold her in his arms again. She danced like a gossamer fairy but the beauty of her body was real enough. What did that extraordinary episode in her apartment really mean? Was Vinca an innocent or an experienced girl? She had been physically docile, but emotionally detached, he now realized with irritation. Perhaps she was a girl who only appreciated male ruthlessness and was left cold by a gentle considerate lover. That was possibly the answer he thought. Her sister's behavior was therefore deliberate, and intended to make him angry so that he would act the part which appealed to Vinca. It could explain why she was so unmoved. Well, it was a part he would be quite happy to play he thought smugly, and it would be an added spur to lovemaking. He congratulated himself on his clever analysis of the situation and planned his conquest of the lovely and intriguing Vinca.

In due course the beautifully engraved invitation cards to the Foreign Office ball were sent out, and Vinca and Syn were very excited when they arrived, especially Syn when she knew Antony had also received one. They both asked the duchess all about it.

"It's a very important social occasion, to which all the best people are invited."

"Who are the best people?" asked Vinca realizing she must be one of them.

"The people that count, darling."

The use of the word "count" in this context was strange to her and she looked puzzled.

"People who count what?"

Vicky sighed.

"It means the most important people."

"Important for what?" asked Syn calmly.

"Their position, of course, those with titles and money, in other words the most successful people."

"And the nicest people," added Vinca innocently.

The duchess smiled warily.

"Not necessarily, I fear. People with the best characters are scattered indiscriminately through all classes, and would be difficult to find. But that won't stop us all having a good time."

The girls were enchanted at the idea of birthday parties, a conception which was entirely new to them. It led to a hurried study of the calendar which ended up in a long discussion of time and the fascinating knowledge that the earth revolved in its orbit round the sun.

Vicky felt quite exhausted by it all and was pleased to escape home. She believed she had reinstigated the affair between Vinca and James, and she hoped it would stop Vinca getting in her way. It was intolerable that the girl should spend so many evenings with them.

Vicky was by now violently in love with John. Ever since that evening in her apartment her dependence on him had grown steadily. She had loved him before but her earlier feelings were a pale image compared with what she now felt. He had gently led her into a world of sensation she had never dreamed existed, the intensity of her emotions had been inconceivable and each meeting bound her to him tighter with the cords of love. She had always considered herself a knowledgeable woman who could experience nothing really new. But he had taken her into a new world of which she knew nothing. She wondered idly if his unique origin had given him some special magic which enabled him to open doors unknown to other men, but she was not seriously interested in thinking it through. Having secured freedom from Vinca's company, all was right with Vicky's world. She sighed contentedly and went to bed.

As the evening of the ball approached the atmosphere became electric with excitement. Syn and

Vinca had been fitted with exotic gowns for the occasion and were longing to wear them. Syn was happy because Antony was taking her, while Vinca was delighted to know that she would be partnered by James Renshaw. Vicky, who was also being specially dressed for the occasion, was contented as these happy arrangements would leave her in sole possession of John.

Syn and Antony dined together every evening and could hardly bear to be out of each other's company. It was while they were having coffee after a particularly pleasant meal in a quiet Soho restaurant that Syn innocently dropped her bombshell.

"We must live near the sea when we are married, darling."

"You are fond of the sea, aren't you?"

She nodded her head.

"I couldn't live away from it."

He lit a cigarette thoughtfully.

"We shall have to live in London, I fear, because of my job."

She looked at him unbelievingly for a moment for he had always agreed to everything she said.

"You don't mean it, Antony."

"I most certainly do."

"But I couldn't go on living in London with all its dirt and noise."

"Other girls do," he said reasonably.

"But I'm not like other girls."

He smiled at her.

"I go all the way with you on that."

"I'm serious, Antony, if you want to marry me we must live by the sea."

He suddenly realized she was deadly serious.

"But why is it so important?" he asked.

She leaned forward and spoke earnestly.

"I was born in the sea, and I must return to it regularly. I couldn't live without doing so."

Antony now felt worried for he didn't consider this normal behavior.

"How could you have been born in the sea, darling?"

"Well, perhaps I wasn't exactly born in it, but I have lived in the sea as long as I can remember."

There was a pause, and he stubbed out his cigarette deliberately.

"You don't mean that literally," he said.

"But I do."

"Do you mean I've fallen in love with a mermaid?" he asked lightly.

"You don't believe me," she said accusingly.

"You must admit it sounds incredible."

"Ask my guardian then."

"Does he believe it?"

"He brought us up in the world beneath the waves."

Antony suddenly remembered her extraordinary exploit off the Scottish coast and the incredible speed at which she swam. However, being a fast swimmer hardly corroborated so strange a story.

"Even if what you say is true you are obviously a normal girl capable of living an ordinary life. We can spend all our holidays by the sea if that would please you."

Tears of frustration appeared in her eyes as she realized he did not believe her.

"That wouldn't be enough," she said.

"Why not?"

She then explained to him about her potential immortality and he realized that his beautiful and beloved Syn was suffering from a delusion. She was perfectly normal in every other way and he would be patient and sympathetic with her. Marriage, he felt certain, would soon banish these extraordinary ideas from her head and he promised to see what he could do in order to pacify her. Antony was nice and understanding as she knew he would be and Syn sighed with relief, however mistaken, at his reasonableness.

But other problems were rapidly developing. Antony's mother, Mrs. Della Watson, arrived home from Jamaica anxious to meet and hear all about the girl her precious son had become engaged to. She listened patiently to Antony for a few minutes.

"Who is her father?" she asked.

"She has no father or mother."

"An orphan," said Della coldly, thinking how much harder it would be to check on such a girl.

"She never knew them, poor dear," said Antony, oblivious of his mother's thoughts. "She has been brought up by her guardian, Sir John Averill."

Della felt her heart give a jump at the name. Her mind flashed back to her youth and her incredible adventures with the golden-headed Triton. She remembered his life in the sea and how eventually his identity had been established. There could be only one man called Sir John Averill.

"Is that the Averill of Electronics Equipment Limited?" she asked.

"That's him."

Before he could ask her any questions she adroitly changed the subject.

"Tell me what Synclaire looks like."

Her mind wondered as he described the charms and virtues of his fiancée. It was a long time since those magic days on Triton's enchanted island where she had taught him to speak the languge of men. She wondered if he was married and what he looked like now. She was in early middle age but had looked after herself. Time had robbed her of her girlish figure but she was still smart and presentable and her eye wandered instinctively to an adjacent mirror.

"Is Sir John Averill married?" she interrupted.

"No, Mother."

"He's a widower then."

"No, he's a bachelor."

So he had never married, she thought, and wondered if it was because of her. They had been very much in love she remembered and the color rose in her face.

"I'm dying to meet Synclaire. She sounds like a perfectly charming girl."

Antony was delighted at her enthusiasm.

"We're all going to the Foreign Office ball."

"Bring your party here for drinks first then. These affairs always start late, and a preliminary warming-up is a great help."

"I'll ask them," said Antony and paused.

His mother looked at him.

"There's one thing that bothers me about Syn," he said diffidently.

"What's that, my dear?"

"She says we must live by the sea when we are married."

"That's not possible with your present job, is it?"

"I know and I've told her, but she insists."

"Did she say why?"

"Yes, Mother," and he poured out the story of Syn's delusions which worried him more than he liked to admit. Della realized with triumph that Syn's guardian could be none other than Triton. Syn obviously knew about his early life and in fantasy was modeling her own on it. The immortality part was just an added frill to make her more important and able to compete with her guardian's abilities.

To Antony's relief Della laughed.

"Young girls are given to fancies. I wouldn't let them upset you. The interest and excitements of marriage will soon wipe them out of her mind and they'll be forgotten."

"Do you think so?" said Antony with relief.

"I'm sure of it, dear boy," and Antony retired to bed feeling greatly reassured.

Vinca and Syn were dressed and looked ravishing. Oswald Raynor was confined to bed but insisted on seeing them before they set off for the ball. They went up for his inspection and he pronounced them the two most beautiful girls in the world, which delighted them. They descended the stairs, the dark beauty of Vinca setting off the blond loveliness of her sister, and found Vicky and John in the dining room where a bottle of iced champagne sat in a silver bucket. Beside it on the table were two small packages.

"A happy birthday to you," said Vicky smiling and kissed them both.

They thanked her for their birthday gifts received that morning, an upper-air custom which they had known nothing about but which they thought delightful.

They approached John shyly. He picked up one package and gave it to Vinca.

"Many happy returns of your birthday, darling," he said and kissed her gently on the mouth.

He repeated the procedure with Syn and Vicky noticed that they both blushed slightly as they opened their presents but her mind was soon diverted by the presents themselves. The two morocco leather boxes were opened and the three of them stood momentarily in stunned silence. Two perfectly graduated diamond necklaces lay scintillating on their white satin beds. Vicky, who had an extensive knowledge of jewelry and precious stones, let out a gasp. They were glorious and, she imagined, almost priceless. The man responsible for cutting them had almost had apoplexy, for in order to achieve the correct graduation he had to cut some of the diamonds to waste, making them smaller than was necessary. He had almost refused to do it. To cut a large diamond down to a smaller one struck him as iniquitous. He of course did not know that John could pick up handfuls of them when required and he had to admit the results were superb when his creation was complete.

When they had caught their breath Syn and Vinca squealed with delight and excitedly put them on and they looked exquisite round their graceful necks. With the excitement bubbling John opened the champagne and the bottle was emptied in honor of the birthday. Not long afterward Antony and James Renshaw arrived and they set off for Antony's home.

Della Watson had dressed herself with care and looked forward with mixed feelings to meeting John

Averill again. She thought of their quarrel years ago and how he had strode angrily down to the sea and her fruitless efforts to catch up with him in the soft sand. She had kicked off her high-heeled shoes to make better progress and could visualize perfectly the evening dress she had worn that evening. John had slid in his magical way beneath the waves and vanished, leaving her weeping at the water's edge. Oddly she remembered her dress had been ruined. The sea was empty in the moonlight and he had vanished as if he had never been, and she had not seen him since that day.

John was unaware that it was Della he was about to meet again. They entered the room and Della paled at the sight of him. Antony introduced them and John looked at her curiously. He doesn't even recognize me she thought and flushed.

Then he put out his hand.

"Della!" he exclaimed.

He held her hand in his for a moment. "What a pleasant surprise after all this time."

She swallowed, still suffering from the shocking surprise of seeing him exactly as he had been when she was a young girl.

"You haven't changed," she said in amazement. Antony had turned aside and they faced each other alone for a moment.

"You're exactly as you used to be," she muttered almost accusingly.

He ignored the observation as if it were of no consequence and smiled.

"I'd no idea you were Antony's mother—you've a very charming son, Della."

She murmured a platitude, still stunned by the

fact that age had not touched him, and a wave of resentment flooded her. The care she had taken over making her toilet suddenly seemed pathetic. She was a middle-aged woman with all that that implied while John stood before her making her look ridiculous—at least in her own eyes and surely in his. She remembered how they had lain in each other's arms on the tropical sands of his Caribbean island, how she had taught him to speak, all his many endearing ways. Without knowing it, she had been romanticizing about this meeting and now she could have wept with frustration. She spoke coldly.

"What's the explanation, John?"

"It's a legacy of the sea."

"Are your wards the same?" she asked flatly.

"I think so, Della. There's no reason why they shouldn't be."

They were joined by the others and Della used the interruption to admire the lovely necklaces, keeping her composure and acting the graceful hostess. No one could have guessed she had just received the shock of her life. When they had all gone she retired to her room and wept bitterly.

The ball was a vastly impressive affair and Syn and Vinca were delighted by its grandeur. They loved the wonderful gowns and jewels of the women, the beribboned men and the band. They were particularly happy with the refreshments.

The girls came as close to causing a riot as the somewhat formal circumstances would permit. There was hardly a man in the room who did not ask for a dance. Vicky was quite put out. If she had not known a lot of those present she would have been at quite a disadvantage, an entirely new experience for her and one she did not like. However she was compensated by having John as her partner and although she had to dance with one or two others or appear rude it did not prevent her from monopolizing him most of the evening.

The amazing necklaces caused a great stir and as most of the great gems and famous pieces are known, one or two knowledgeable individuals wondered for a moment if they might be fakes, for they were certainly dramatic enough to be known. Oswald Raynor when he saw them said they should be named but John had only laughed. They were a source of conversation at the supper tables where they caused a lot of talk and speculation. A famous fashion writer devoted most of her article to them in the press the next day. She had asked the girls if they were known by any name and on the spur of the moment John said they were the Sesame diamonds—which was to cause them all a lot of trouble in the near future.

Vicky actually enjoyed herself immensely until almost the end of the evening. She noted with pleasure that the girls danced with almost everyone except John. He suddenly felt his finger tingle and retreated to a quiet corner where Syn's voice whispered in his ear.

"We've kept the last two dances for you."

"Where are you?"

"In the powder room."

He chuckled.

"I'll be seeing you," he said.

He told Vicky, who wondered how it had been arranged. They had not spoken to each other all the evening so it must have been planned before they came.

"Drat those girls," she thought.

She did not wish to be a wallflower at the end of the evening and wondered momentarily if the information had been withheld until the last moment for that very reason, but quickly banished the unworthy thought. It would be entirely out of character. Love was making her jealous and suspicious. It was funny how a virtue could produce vice she thought as she casually drifted round the room and gracefully accepted partners for the last two dances. There was still the peculiar incident at the supper table to be explained and she intended to question Vinca later. She had asked her for the salt and Vinca had passed it to her saying: "There you are, bitch," while giving her a charming smile.

Everyone had looked up from their plates in the sudden silence while James Renshaw, who had just taken a mouthful of soup, nearly blew it out again. He had retained it with difficulty but in doing so had forced some of it up the back of his throat and for one ghastly moment wondered if it would come out of his nose. Fortunately he only suffered acute discomfort.

Vicky had paled slightly but otherwise had taken it in her stride and thanking Vinca had continued with her supper as if nothing unusual had occurred, leaving her neighbors wondering if they had heard aright. Conversation had soon filled the silence, leaving the majority wondering what Vinca had really said.

When Antony arrived home there was a note from his mother asking him to see her before he went to bed. It was late and he crept upstairs but there was a light under her door and he found her reading. She had found sleep impossible and could not concentrate on her book. As well as being emotionally disturbed herself she was worried about Antony. What would happen if he married this girl Syn. She was undoubtedly a beauty and charming into the bargain, and by virtue of her necklace alone a very wealthy girl. But supposing what John had said was true; she knew him well enough to know he would not lie unless time had changed his character completely. Besides which he had nothing to gain by doing so.

He might be mistaken of course, but supposing he was not. It would mean this girl would remain young and beautiful while Antony slowly became an old man, as she had become an old woman. Tears of mortification welled in her eyes and for the first time in her life she faced the fact of age and feared it. The slow, inevitable crumbling of body and mind was a terrible sentence imposed on the human race. She wished it were possible to remain in one's prime and having completed the allotted span of life die cleanly and suddenly.

There was a tap on the door.

"Come in."

"It's late, Mother, you should be asleep."

She made up her mind. "I've something to tell you, Antony."

He sat on the edge of the bed and yawned.

"It's about Syn."

He was immediately all attention.

"Sir John Averill and I are old friends. We were in love with each other once in our youth."

He looked at her in surprise.

"It's difficult to believe, isn't it, when he looks so young."

Antony nodded his head.

"I've never told you the story, but I will now," she said and he was gaping at her when she had finished.

"What is he then?"

"He's a human being, but very different from us. Living in the sea like that has given him some form of longevity. Don't ask me how but it's a fact. He's exactly the same now as when I was a young girl."

"What about Syn?"

"He thinks she is the same. I asked him."

"So it's not a delusion."

"No, and if you marry her you must be resigned to slowly growing old while she remains as she is now."

"It's impossible."

Della shrugged her shoulders.

"There are four people who could verify the facts, if they are still alive. Oswald Raynor, the banker——"

"They are staying in his house," interrupted Antony. She nodded.

"The others are Dr. Crane, the marine biologist, Captain Ferguson and Dr. Ryall."

"I can hardly believe it," he muttered.

"I'm sorry, Antony, but those are the facts and it's important you should know them."

"Thank you, Mother," he said and kissing her he abruptly left the room, a confused and bewildered young man.

Triton was basically kind in spite of the ruthless

environment in which he had been bred. He had seen the shock in Della's eyes on meeting him and had sensed the pain beneath it. She had been his first love and being empathic he could put himself in her place and almost feel as she did. He had been appalled at the emotions this evoked. He thought of her several times during the evening and grieved for her sadness. He rang her up the next morning and after a slight hesitation she agreed to have lunch with him. He took her to a quiet restaurant where they had a table in a small alcove.

"Do you still like pink gin?"

"Fancy remembering after all this time," she said in a pleased voice.

He smiled at her.

"You were not an easy person to forget, Della."

The waiter brought their drinks.

"What cigarettes would you like?"

"I have some," she said opening her bag and bringing out her case. She helped herself to one and looked at him questioningly.

"You haven't changed your habits?" she queried. He shook his head.

"You see I haven't forgotten either."

He noticed the flame of the lighter trembled slightly as she lit her cigarette.

"I shall never forget that terrible evening," she said in a low voice.

"I was very young and inexperienced, Della, and when I saw you kissing Mark I assumed you'd discarded me."

"If I'd only been able to run a little faster and catch up with you I could have explained everything."

He leaned forward and looked at her earnestly.

"Seeing me now, Della, are you pleased or sorry?"

She had been young and impressionable and losing him in that way had been a great grief to her. She had regretted that evening all her life, and even when happily married she had often thought of him. Suddenly the implication of his question hit her. Looking at the vibrant youth gazing at her across the table she wondered. Supposing they had married as they had intended, what would her feelings be like now? He could almost be taken for her son she thought, and suddenly felt a lightening of her old sorrow.

"I know what you mean," she said.

"Say it, Della."

She looked at him steadily.

"I would never have believed it but you're right. I'm glad we never married—very glad," she added.

He lifted his glass and drank to her silently.

"I owe you a lot, Della, and I'm grateful to you— you were my first love," he said softly.

She touched his hand with a trembling little smile and then rummaged in her hand bag for a hanky and dabbed her eyes. He had cured her ache and smoothed away her resentment and she suddenly felt lighthearted and even gay.

They had a pleasant meal reminiscing over the past and more than one diner wondered who the handsome woman was with the infectious laugh.

"What about Syn and Antony?"

John shrugged his shoulders.

"You've told Antony?"

She nodded.

"What else can you do?" he said.

"I'm worried about him."

"I'm sure you are, Della, and I'm equally concerned about Syn. They both understand the situation, however, and must make their own decisions. We can do no more."

"I suppose not," she said frowning and remembered with misgivings how she had felt in a similar situation. No one had known then about Triton's longevity and she wondered if it would have made any difference if she had. She doubted it.

chapter seven

A MASSIVELY BUILT MAN called Rodique skimmed through the morning papers while smoking his after-breakfast cigar. A dainty Chinese girl dressed in an aquamarine kimono with a large golden dragon on its back stood behind him kneading his thick bull neck, her slender fingers almost disappearing into the rolls of fat.

Rodique glanced at the social news and with a grunt he carefully read the article about the two diamond necklaces. He had already met Averill and was curious about his diamond mine. Rereading the report with satisfaction he picked up the phone and asked for a New York number. He spoke to the chief manager of one of his shipping interests and ordered the girl out of the room.

"Use the scrambler, Vincent," he said and switched on his own.

"What news about Averill's mine?"

"We arranged for Kurt to investigate but he seems to have disappeared."

"What do you mean seems to, has he or hasn't he?"

"We can't contact him. I flew a man out to investigate and Kurt has vanished."

"Why didn't you say so in the first place," said Rodique curtly.

"Sorry, Mr. Rodique."

"Averill has slipped up and unwittingly given us a clue. The diamonds come from a cave."

"A cave, Mr. Rodique?"

"That's what I said, and I've no doubt it's somewhere on his Caribbean island. I don't want any more mincing about. Get hold of Burchard and tell him to take a team there. I want every inch of that island combed until we find what we want. It should be a simple procedure. The place is miles from anywhere and no one will know what happens."

"Yes, Mr. Rodique."

"Tell him to take skin divers. If they can't find it on the island I want them to search for an underwater entrance. Tell Burchard to stay there until he finds the mine."

"Yes, Mr. Rodique."

The big man slammed the phone down in irritation. Vincent got under his skin with his "Yes, Mr. Rodique," and "No, Mr. Rodique." He let out a bellow.

"Sue."

The girl hurried in, her small feet tapping anxiously on the parquet floor.

"Get on with it," he growled.

Burchard was a professional crook—a man whose appearance belied his physical condition. There was no weapon or method of destruction which he was not either familiar with or adept at. He was thin and sallow-faced, his motivating force was greed and his pale slate-colored eyes regarded his fellow creatures without emotion. He chose five men as hard and as tough as himself. Each possessed a special ability and was familiar in the use of the aqualung. Johnson was an electrical expert, and another a master of automatic weapons. A third specialized in explosives while a fourth could open any combination lock with his sensitive fingers and the help of a stethoscope. The fifth was a karate expert.

This was the team that Burchard took to Crab Island and they entered the lagoon and disembarked on the sandy shore on a fine peaceful afternoon. They scattered silently and approached the house like commandos, only to find it empty. They faded away rapidly, disappearing among the trees, and when they shortly returned they knew there was no one else on the island.

"A bit of luck," said Burchard when he had received their reports.

One of the men wiped the sweat from his forehead and another spat.

"We'll make our headquarters here. Four of you unload the boat and you, Johnson, come with me."

The locked front door presented no problems and they searched the house thoroughly while Burchard decided where the men would sleep. He chose the master bedroom for himself and was admiring the bathroom when a puzzled Johnson appeared.

"There's something damn queer going on here," he said.

"What's that," asked Burchard sharply.

Instead of answering Johnson walked over to the bath and turned on the hot-water tap.

"Well, I'm damned," he said as it came out hot.

"What are you talking about?" said Burchard coldly.

"There's a deepfreeze in the kitchen full of food and the water's hot."

"What the hell's wrong with that?"

"There's no bloody power source."

There was a moment's dead silence.

"You must be wrong."

"Come and see for yourself, there's no power cable running to the deepfreeze and I bet the water is heated by a coil also without a power source."

Burchard was thorough and painstaking, a man who left nothing to chance, and he soon verified what Johnson had said. The radiotelephone was the same. They could think of no possible explanation and Burchard, who liked nothing that could not be explained, felt uneasy. What sort of place was this and who was the man who owned it, he wondered, and he had a sudden premonition of disaster which he quickly shook off. With his hand-picked team he had nothing to fear.

They moved their stores, settled themselves comfortably into the house and set up a lookout rotation schedule. They then started a systematic examination of the island but discovered nothing, not even a cave to explore. The search then extended to the seabed, and the aqualung divers went down, and found there were many grottoes and caves in the foundations of Crab Island but none that contained any diamonds.

Lord James Renshaw was pleased with his own

perspicacity. His analysis of the situation with regard to Vinca he considered masterly and he undoubtedly had a wide experience in the ways of the world and of women. Vinca was a charming little thing who required a domineering and imperious male before she could react. It was a role he flattered himself he could easily fill. Her resistance would crumble and she would fall willingly into his arms and he might even consider marrying her.

Vinca was delighted when he rang up and asked if she would like a trip in his launch.

"Will you take me out to sea, James?"

"I could take you to France if necessary."

He drove her to Richmond and taking a large picnic lunch aboard they started off downriver. She was full of curiosity and asked a spate of questions which he enjoyed answering. How alive and vital she is, he thought. He watched her curiously as they left the river mouth and met the waves of the English Channel. She leaned forward eagerly as if returning home after a long absence. Vinca was delighted to be at sea again and suddenly realized how much she had missed it. The green depths and white-capped waves were home and she almost wept with pleasure. Her enjoyment would have been complete if only Triton and Syn had been with them. She wondered why they had not thought of doing this before and decided the three of them must do it regularly in the future.

James intended to travel well out of sight of land so that Vinca would feel helpless and at his mercy. They opened the hamper and had a pleasant lunch of cold chicken and champagne. The launch drove steadily onward until they were alone between sea and sky. Then James cut the motor. The sudden silence produced a sense of isolation. They were alone in the world except for the green waves, and there was no sound but for the occasional lap of water against the sides of the boat.

"You can't get away from me now, Vinca."

His words hardly made sense to her, and she looked at him questioningly.

"Your sister won't be able to interrupt us this time," he said.

"Did that upset you, James?"

"What do you think?"

"Everyone is not the same," she said, thinking of the dolphins.

"I intend to start where we left off," he said watching her.

She shook her head and smiled.

"I mean what I say," he said ominously.

"You wouldn't do it against my will?"

"I most certainly shall," he said beginning to feel angry.

Vinca was shocked, for this was an alien concept to her. No creature in the sea, however ruthless or predatory, would ever attempt to make love by force. She could hardly believe she had heard aright.

"You wouldn't," she said outraged.

His answer was to cross the boat and grab her. He seized her in his arms and kissed her roughly.

"Are you going to make a fight of it?"

She shook her head weakly, tears in her eyes. She wept because her image of James was broken and could never be repaired. Some of the tears were for herself at her own loss for she imagined herself in love with him.

"Do you want my clothes off?" she asked innocently. His mouth felt dry as he said yes and stepped back to watch. She deftly slipped out of her things until she was standing only in her bra and panties, and she looked at him intently for a moment.

"Goodbye, James," she said gravely and diving neatly overboard vanished. Taken by surprise he rushed to the side of the boat but she was nowhere in sight.

He suddenly laughed and sitting down lit a cigarette. She would have to come back for there was nowhere she could go. He smoked leisurely, waiting for her to make the first move. The cigarette was finished and still there was no sign of her. He looked round at an empty sea and then grinned. She was very likely holding on to the bows of the boat in order to give him a scare. He would soon deal with that. He glanced over the stern just to make sure for he did not want to chew her up with the propeller, and starting the engines he put the boat full speed astern. She would be unable to hang on and he searched forward expecting to see her head appear any moment. Still no girlish figure waved or shouted at him indignantly. He cut the engines and looked around anxiously, wondering where she could be, but the sea remained a waste, empty of life except for himself. As time slowly passed his anxiety turned to fear and he shouted out her name repeatedly. When he had fruitlessly yelled himself hoarse he sat down and put his head in his hands with a groan. What had he done? He searched the sea with binoculars until darkness prevented him and it was not until then he admitted to himself that Vinca was drowned, and that he was responsible for her death.

Pale-faced with shock and remorse he made for home.

Vinca entered her natural habitat with delight. She arrowed down to the seabed and leveling off swam at speed. The sandy floor fled beneath her and she began to call out in the high fluting notes of Dolphinese. But there was no answer for this was not dolphin country and it seemed strange to her to swim in a silent sea when she was accustomed to the chattering of the dolphins always about her. She found the Channel sparse in life compared with the Caribbean and missed the brilliant-hued fish, the seaweeds and the corals of her home waters. She thought of James with sorrow and then banished him from her mind. She surfaced some miles away and utilizing the dolphin lore of the sea turned unerringly for the river. She was not hungry and made no attempt to feed on the fish she passed. It was a fine calm afternoon when she reached the river mouth, traveling at speed some six feet below the surface. The water however became so murky that she was forced to swim more or less on the surface. Owing to the perfect conditions she was picked up on the Cliff radar, chiefly because of her speed, for she showed up only as a faint and irregular trace on the screen.

"What do you make of that, Jack?"

"Something small, but it's moving at a hell of a lick." The observer phoned the radar at Gravesend.

"Something coming up the river at speed," he said.

"What is it?"

"Some kind of fish I should think."

"Fish," said the voice derisively, "since when have you got fish on radar?"

The observer said a few lurid words and then dialed the Thames Navigational Service at the Royal Terrace Pier and was put on to the harbor master.

"Something small and fast coming up the river," he reported and hung up quickly before he could be asked any silly questions. Vinca passed the pier at speed, and was watched through binoculars.

"What the devil is it?"

She was difficult to see as she fled forward with a sinuous motion for the water kept breaking over her as she repeatedly surfaced.

"The motion reminds me of a dolphin," said the older man uncertainly.

"It's wearing something."

"Probably a patch of white skin."

"It looks almost human to me."

"Not swimming at that speed, sonny, unless it's a mermaid!" Both of them watched intently until Vinca was out of sight. The older man phoned the Port of London Authority and warned them.

"What is it?" he was asked.

"I've no idea, but it's going like a bomb."

"What's it look like?"

"A mermaid," he said grinning and hung up smartly.

This facetious remark was ignored but the harbor service launches were warned to keep a lookout for an unknown object traveling fast upriver.

The water was foul and Vinca increased her speed to maximum and as this was over twenty-five knots she left a considerable wake behind her. The sooner she got out of this filthy river the better, she thought.

She shot past Tilbury Docks and took the curve of the river close to the shore as she entered Galleons Reach. As she shot at speed along the straight stretch of Woolwich Reach she was seen with disbelief by the crew of an occasional ship and people on the riverside wharfs. The press and the Thames Division of the Metropolitan Police began to receive excited telephone calls, each of which varied in its description of the rapidly moving creature. Obviously something unusual was happening and patrol craft were notified while editors sent reporters posthaste to the river. The news of Vinca traveled ahead of her and there were soon observers on the riverbanks. Tower Bridge became jammed with sightseers who gathered a mermaid was swimming upriver at a prodigious rate. They stood staring expectantly while rumors spread like forest fires. It was a pity that Quebec Dock was below the bridge and not above it for the crowd would have had a perfect view of Vinca tearing through the water at an incredible speed below them, but it was an experience they were to be denied.

She shot round the curve of Greenwich Reach and was spotted from Greenwich Pier. A patrol launch went after her and soon there were several craft following in her wake. Some of the observers noted the creature appeared to be wearing panties and could hardly believe their eyes. Some thought it human, having glimpsed a face, but could see no arms.

Vinca slowed at the commencement of Limehouse Reach and angled left through the entrance to Greenland Dock. The pursuing boats continued up Limehouse Reach and by the time they had reached the lower pool realized they had missed her. Some continued on more slowly, while others turned back searching the river closely. There was a cry of triumph from one boat whose crew saw a long object floating half submerged near the bank but it was only a tree trunk.

Vinca submerged and passed under the swing bridge into Canada Dock. As she entered Quebec Dock she surfaced and gave a high-pitched fluting whistle. Nero, who was on deck, ran to the stern and threw the waiting rope ladder overboard and Vinca ran up it like a monkey. She smiled at the astonished man and making straight for the bathroom spent an hour in hot soapy water before she felt clean again.

John was about to leave his office when he felt the telltale tingle in his finger and twisted the ring.

"Who is it?"

"Vinca," said a breathless little voice. "Please send the car for me."

John smiled.

"Where are you?"

"On the *Poseidon*."

John's face showed surprise.

"What are you doing down there?" he asked.

"Something dreadful has happened, I'll tell you when I see you."

"You all right, Vinca?"

"Yes, but I do want to see you."

"I'll come right away."

He drove down himself and entered the main saloon calling out her name. She flew in, flung her arms round him and burst into tears. He stroked her hair and soothed her, wondering what on earth had happened.

"Let's sit down and you can tell me all about it."

She climbed onto his lap like a little girl and told him the whole story.

"I could never love him now," she sobbed.

"Growing up is a painful business, Vinca, but at least you know where you are."

"But it was so much nicer before I did."

"You don't want to live in a fool's paradise."

"Of course not," she said indignantly.

"James is obviously not for you, my dear."

"But I don't know anyone else who might want to give me a ring," she wailed.

"There's plenty of time for that, Vinca," he said sharply. "You're not a child now though you are behaving like one." Her tear-stained face looked at him in hurt surprise.

"Antony only gave your sister a ring as a symbol of their love for each other. It's the love that is important, not the ring."

Vinca nodded her head contritely.

"I know that," she murmured.

"There are plenty of other men in the world besides James."

"Suppose they're all like him," she said in sudden dismay.

John laughed.

"I never want to see him again," she said emphatically.

"Can you imagine what his feelings are now, Vinca?"

She looked puzzled.

"He'll think you're drowned."

"Why should he?" she said in surprise.

"No earth girl out of sight of land could swim home like that."

Vinca perked up and managed to look faintly superior.

"He'll be in a terrible state of mind," said John thoughtfully.

"Serve him right," she said with satisfaction.

He slapped her small rump.

"Let's go home, you little savage."

She jumped off his lap indignantly and they returned to the car.

"What will he do?" she asked as they drove off.

"He's almost certain to come and tell me about it."

Vinca giggled.

"What's funny about that?"

"It will be amusing to hear him describe my death."

The phone rang as they entered the house and John picked it up.

"Who is it?" asked Vinca.

John covered the mouthpiece.

"It's Renshaw," he whispered.

Vinca waited impatiently and thought the conversation would never end. At last John hung up.

"Well!" she said.

"He's very upset."

"So he should be," said Vinca feelingly.

"He's driving over here now."

Vinca grimaced and vanished upstairs.

Renshaw was still shocked and grieved over Vinca's death. He pondered over what he would say as he drove over. There would be no need to go into the actual details, he thought. On arrival he was shown immediately into the study.

"Sit down, you look as if you could do with a drink," said John and poured him out a stiff whisky.

Renshaw was relieved at the calm way Sir John appeared to be taking it and gratefully gulped some down.

"Tell me what happened," said John.

"There's not much more to say, sir. Vinca said she wanted to swim and simply dived overboard and vanished."

Vinca who had been listening through a partly opened door of the adjacent room, walked in indignantly.

"You're a liar, James. I never said that."

John was pleased she had not prolonged the agony.

James Renshaw sat petrified for a moment, the color draining from his face. He rose shakily.

"Thank God you're alive," he said thickly. "But how . . . ?"

He looked from one to the other of them in the ensuing silence.

"I'm neither a wanted nor a worthy guest," he muttered and turning he left the room while Vinca burst into tears.

James Renshaw returned home with his emotions in a turmoil. Uppermost was the great relief that Vinca was alive, although he could not imagine how it was possible. He was full of shame and remorse at his behavior and realized he had entirely misjudged the situation. For once he could not fully evaluate the facts and he wondered what these two girls were really like. He could find no possible explanation for

110

their behavior in the flat that night. His ego had suffered greatly during his interview with Sir John and the arrival of Vinca. He had never been in such a humiliating position in the whole of his well-ordered and polished life. He resented the poor figure he had cut and the feelings of guilt he had experienced. Almost as if I were a criminal he thought savagely. Now that Vinca appeared beyond his grasp he suddenly realized how fond of her he was. He had never met anyone who had appealed to him so much and to his consternation began to wonder if he was in love with her.

He tossed and turned all night thinking about her and the next morning as early as he decently could he telephoned. She was rather cool and refused to have dinner with him but after much persuasion she agreed to meet him for coffee that morning. She was subdued and silent and he did not see her enthusiasm return until the arrival of the cream cakes. She chose two after careful consideration, and ate them with relish.

She looked at him and smiled for the first time.

"They're lovely, why don't you have one?"

He shook his head.

"Do you mind if I smoke?"

"Of course not," she said between mouthfuls.

He lowered his voice.

"I want to apologize, I don't know what made me do it."

Her blue eyes regarded him steadily.

"Don't you, James?"

Suddenly he realized there was only one Vinca in the world and that he very much wanted her. He heard himself saying abruptly, "I love you, Vinca."

111

"You'd never have behaved like that if you did."

"That is why I did it," he said stubbornly, peeved at her reaction.

"You're randy, James, that's the real reason."

He flushed at the word and saw a cup of coffee at the adjacent table stop dead, halfway to its owner's mouth. He glanced round the room which was full of women whom he could imagine listening to them.

"Keep your voice down," he hissed, "and don't use vulgar words."

"It's in the Oxford Dictionary, randy—meaning lustful."

"Have you finished?"

"Yes, James," she said demurely.

They left the shop in silence and parted outside. Vinca took a taxi, while James walked moodily down Piccadilly toward Green Park.

chapter eight

ANTONY WATSON was a confused and unhappy young man. He had to believe what his mother had told him about Sir John Averill and herself, though the story seemed incredible. What was true for Sir John, however, need not necessarily apply to his ward. He was sure Synclaire was a perfectly normal girl. In love with her as he was he could not bear to think otherwise. He arranged to take her out for dinner that evening and worried about it all day. It was a quiet, discreet restaurant where each table was illuminated with its own small lamp. They sat in a secluded corner and had an excellent meal, though Antony hardly noticed the taste of the various dishes.

"Did you know that your guardian and my mother were friends when they were young?"

Syn nodded her head.

"He told me."

"You wouldn't think so to look at them now."

"I agree," said Syn calmly.

"How do you account for it then?"

She looked at him thoughtfully.

"It's a gift of the sea," she said quietly.

"What is, Syn?" he said looking at her intently.

"Longevity, or as John puts it, potential immortality. Nothing grows old in the sea, Antony."

"Is that why you don't want to leave it?"

"Partly, but chiefly because it's home and I couldn't bear to be away from it for long."

His mouth felt dry and he swallowed.

"Will you continue to remain young like you are now?"

Syn could sense that Antony was under stress. He seemed apprehensive and worried but she failed to realize the reason. She looked at him anxiously.

"Well?" he repeated.

"John thinks so, Antony."

He sighed and took a drink of wine.

"Suppose you never saw the sea again, would it still apply?"

She shrugged her shoulders.

"I don't know, perhaps not."

"But of course you want immortality," he said harshly.

"I don't want to grow old and wrinkled if that's what you mean," she said.

"But you don't mind if I do?"

Tears welled in her eyes and he instinctively put his hand over hers.

"I'm sorry, Syn, I didn't mean that."

She began to realize for the first time that prolonged youth was more likely to engender envy than admiration.

The dinner with Syn left Antony acutely depressed. He must thrash out the whole problem so that he knew where he stood. Antony was not a young man who could stand uncertainty. He immediately arranged to see Sir John Averill. He came to the point at once, repeated what his mother and Syn had told him and asked if it was true.

"It's true for me as you can see, and since Syn and Vinca have led the same life, I assume it will apply to them also."

"Would it make any difference if they left the sea?"

"It might well do so but only time could answer that question for you."

Antony remained silent and thoughtful.

"What's worrying you?" John asked.

"How would you like a wife who remained young and beautiful while you grew old?" Antony flashed resentfully.

"If you love Syn more than yourself it should be an added attraction," John said quietly.

Antony rose with some indignation.

"You can never be in a position to judge that, sir," he said and took his leave.

At this crucial point for Antony he was offered a promotion. It would mean going to Germany where the parent firm had its main factory. The offer was too good to turn down and it helped him make up his mind about Syn, for if he accepted the job it meant leaving immediately. In a sense he was running from the problem, at best leaving it in Syn's lap. He told himself that she had to make the decision anyway.

He wrote a long letter to Syn, packed his bags, said goodbye to his mother and took the next plane.

He saw England spread below him with its toy towns and thin connecting ribbons of road. As he crossed the Channel and left it behind him he thought of Syn down there, a dot among all the other specks of humanity. He had made his gesture and it was now up to her. He reasoned that she either loved him enough or she did not.

Syn received his letter the next day and was stunned. She hastened to John, pale-faced and tearless.

"Whatever's the matter?" he asked with concern. Stony-faced she handed him the letter.

Dear Syn,

When you read this I shall be in the heart of Germany far from the sea. I was offered promotion which necessitated immediate acceptance and decided to take it.

I have at last, though with difficulty, come to accept the incredible facts of your life. I do not think you realize what it means emotionally to a man to realize that his beautiful wife may retain her youth while he grows old. It is a fearful thought. In marriage everything should be shared and husband and wife should grow old gracefully together. If the years left you unchanged I should eventually be mistaken for your father and if I lived long enough perhaps even for your grandfather. I could not expect you to go on loving an old man and an unbridgeable gulf would slowly divide us.

After talking with your guardian I think there may be a chance that you would live a normal lifespan if you never again enter the sea. If you love me enough to take this course of action I am more than willing to take the risk involved.

I realize I'm asking you to give up something no human being has ever had before, something which you may well find precious and I shall understand and sympathize with whatever decision you make.

Do not think too hardly of me for presenting you with such a choice for whether we meet again or not I shall always be your very loving Antony.

John looked up at her when he had finished reading. Very gently he took her hand. Her eyes welled with tears.

"Come and sit down," he said kindly.

She sat on his lap and burying her face in his shoulder and sobbed her heart out.

He stroked her golden hair abstractedly, murmuring and patting gently to soothe her. To a certain degree he could not help a feeling of guilt for her distress—but on the other hand he knew enough of men to realize that both Syn and Vinca had been unlucky.

"I d-don't know what to do," Syn mumbled.

"He should never have given her such a wicked choice," said Vinca who had accompanied her sister and now stood white-faced and angry.

"I l-love him s-so," sobbed Syn.

"Of course you do, my dear, but you cannot decide anything when you feel like this," said John.

"Fancy forbidding her ever to go home, never to swim with us beneath the waves again," said Vinca in a shocked voice.

Syn sat up and dabbed her eyes.

"I couldn't give that up either," her sister continued.

"You have both suffered in this city of men. It is no place for us just now."

Both girls looked at him intently.

"We'll go home to the Caribbean where Syn can make up her mind at leisure."

Syn smiled through her tears, and Vinca clapped her hands.

"Let's go now," she said eagerly.

"What about it, Syn?" asked John.

"I don't want to stay here without Antony."

"That's settled then," said John firmly.

He bundled them back to their apartment to pack while he did the same. In spite of Syn's grief he felt lighthearted at the thought of returning to Sea Mount.

First he telephoned Captain McPherson who delightedly made arrangements to sail on the next convenient tide. He then rang up Vicky who swore under her breath when she heard the news. It was a most inopportune time to lose him.

"Are the girls going with you?" she asked, hoping he might invite her as well.

"We're all going, Vicky."

"I envy you the trip, have a nice time," she said sweetly and bit her lip with vexation as she hung up, wondering how long it would be before she saw him again. John took his leave of Raynor who was now a little better, unaware that he would never see the old man again and then phoned Dr. Cunningham and told him his plans. By evening they were all aboard and they slipped quietly down the river on the early morning tide.

It was misty, and small beads of water lined the rigging, but the mist cleared and blew away as they entered the Channel. The sun climbed above the horizon like a big scarlet ball and momentarily painted the sails a rosy red. The three of them leaned over the rail relieved at their separation from high-pressured, ambiguous humanity and already anticipating the freedom of their natural habitat.

They beat their way up the Channel, passing Dieppe, Cherbourg and then the Channel Islands. They rounded Brest and entered the Bay of Biscay from where they struck out across the Atlantic. They would not see land again until they passed the Azores.

As they entered the Bay of Biscay the sun shone out of a cloudless sky. McPherson stood at the wheel, a cheroot between his teeth and a contented look on his face. The *Poseidon* glided forward silently except for the occasional hum of wind in her rigging. Neither John nor the two girls had eaten natural food now for some time and John suddenly felt a craving for it. Sprats were a favorite delicacy and they were to be found here in the bay. He looked at his two young companions.

"Sprats," he said smiling and made for his cabin.

He returned to the deck equipped to enter his domain wearing shorts and knuckle-dusters of golden metal. The girls joined him attired in bras and panties of the same substance. He ran down the poop deck and swallow-dived over the stern with Syn and Vinca on either side of him. They plunged down deep, clouds of small air bubbles escaping from their hair, and began to range the ocean, remaining perfectly spaced like the dolphins they so closely simulated. Triton was in the lead with a girl on either side of him; their heads at the level of his shoulders they swept forward turning and twisting as one unit. They reveled in the play of their muscles and fled through the sea at maximum speed swooping and curving round the bay like a great three-engined plane.

They only broke formation when they spied a shoal of silvery sprats and began to feed after which they joined up again. They saw some pilchards and darted happily after them. The bay was not as beautiful as their Caribbean hunting grounds to which they were longing to return, but for the moment it would more than suffice.

"Think of dirty old London now," piped Vinca joyfully. Syn swam fast turning and twisting as if trying to escape from herself. She felt happier in this silent green world than she had since receiving Antony's letter. It acted like a balm, soothing her frayed nerves. She could not contemplate giving it up and wondered how Antony could ever have asked her to do such a thing. She shot to the surface to breathe, arching out of the water in a parabola and reentering the water silently. If Antony had only experienced the pleasure and wonder of this existence where gravity was banished and speed effortless he would never have asked her to leave it. What was he doing now, she wondered, deep in the heart of Germany and far from the ocean that was her real home. Unable to see the other two she called out in Dolphinese and making in the general direction of the answering calls soon caught up with them.

They swam as one, the girls' hair streaming out behind them. They swooped and curved round the bay, arching out of the water like huge fish when they needed to inhale and reveling in speed and the ecstasy of physical effort.

Captain McPherson handed over the wheel to Mr. Greenway and was leaning over the rail when they returned. He watched their slender bodies cleaving effortlessly through the water and wondered again how they achieved such speed with so little apparent motion. They swarmed up the rope ladder one after the other and went to their cabins. McPherson looked at his watch. They had been out over six hours and looked as fresh as if they had just woken up.

Day after day they sailed across the Atlantic wastes and when the wind failed McPherson used the powerful engines which could pluck unlimited power from the air.

The *Poseidon* made good time and was already in her home waters when a warning was broadcast to all shipping. Captain McPherson approached Triton, grim-faced, and sat down beside him.

"You're looking very serious for such a lovely day," said Triton.

"There's a report of subterranean volcanic activity somewhere between St. John's and the Azores."

"That's a good way away, isn't it?"

Captain McPherson nodded his head.

There was silence for a moment.

"You're worried about it?"

"It's a possible tsunami, I fear," replied the captain.

"What's that?"

McPherson looked at him in mild surprise.

"It's a seismic wave born in the deep trenches of the ocean floor. The ocean bed at those depths is in a state of uneasy equilibrium due to the internal pressure of the earth below and the great pressure of water above. A slight shift of that equilibrium and a great destructive wave suddenly rises out of the sea, and is called a tsunami."

"Could one be on the way?"

McPherson hesitated.

"Perhaps, but there is no tsunami warning system in the Caribbean like there is in the Pacific Ocean."

"How high could such a wave be?" asked Triton after a pause.

"About two feet in the open sea."

Triton looked astonished.

"It's their speed and length that counts. They travel very fast and their crests are far apart."

McPherson relit his cheroot before continuing.

"On April first, nineteen forty-six, there was volcanic activity in one of the deep trenches near the island of Unmak in the Aleutian chain of islands off Alaska. The waves were only two feet high but they traveled at four hundred and seventy miles an hour and their crests were ninety miles apart. When they hit the coasts of Hawaii two thousand miles away the water rose twenty-five feet above normal level and you can imagine the irresistible force of such a mass of water traveling at that speed. Buildings and people were destroyed without warning in seconds. There is a system of observers in the Pacific, and coasts can now be warned at what time such a wave will strike them and they have time to evacuate."

Triton sat up suddenly.

"Is that likely to happen here?"

McPherson shrugged his shoulders.

"It could. I imagine the severity might depend on which side of the Atlantic ridge the wave originates."

Triton looked puzzled.

"Below the Atlantic and running southward from Iceland to within a short distance of Antarctica is a well-defined central ridge, the curve of which follows the line of the African coast. It's really a mountain chain and only surface water on either side of this submarine barrier can cross it."

"If the wave starts on the other side you think it might protect us," said Triton.

"Perhaps, but I don't know enough to be certain."

There was a gentle swell and a breeze that drove the *Poseidon* forward at an easy pace. The sun shone out of an almost cloudless sky and except for the occasional creak of the rigging all was quiet. But it was a deceptive peace as McPherson well knew. The ocean suddenly disturbed in its depths could vomit waves that traveled silently and unseen to break irresistibly upon the land, sweeping beaches and harbors clear of life and carrying large ships far inland.

Triton looked at the calm blue sea. No one knew its ruthlessness better than he did. It was almost a live thing with its doldrum calms and outbursts of hurricane fury. He thought of the great river currents, the intermittent rise and fall of vast masses of warm and cold water and the deep undersea waves, and now the tsunami, a facet of its character he had not known.

They were in sight of Crab Island when further information was received. The epicenter of the earthquake was in the northern extremity of the deep underwater basin of Cape Verde. These vast depressions in the ocean floor form the deepest pits on the surface of the globe. They have been in abysmal darkness since creation and no faintest trace of light has ever touched them since the beginning of the world. Pressed upon from above by millions of tons of water and from below by the internal pressures of the earth the seabed is buckled and warped and such places are the breeding grounds of earthquakes. Already the coasts of France, Spain and Portugal had been inundated by the greatest waves in recorded history and the damage had been colossal.

"We must keep at sea until it's over," said McPherson. Sails were furled and the ship slowly lost speed.

Triton looked at Crab Island, so tantalizingly close.

"How long will it be?" he asked.

McPherson took him to the chartroom. He marked the position of the ship and the reported site of the volcanic disturbance.

"It's approximately three thousand miles from our present position. If we estimate the speed of the tsunami at five hundred miles an hour to be on the safe side, it will reach us in six hours."

"What about Crab Island?"

"It might well be inundated."

"And the house?"

McPherson hesitated.

"It could be destroyed," he said reluctantly.

Triton turned away and looked at the deceptive calmness of the sea. He loved Sea Mount, for it was the one place above the ocean he regarded as home.

He leaned over the rail and gazing at the calm blue Caribbean wondered what it would do to his island. He consoled himself with the thought that he could always rebuild the house and that vegetation would quickly grow again. He did not know the fierce possessiveness of men and as a consequence would not feel the same pangs of loss if Sea Mount was destroyed.

There were, however, several things in the house he sentimentally valued because they had belonged to his parents. They would be irreplaceable if lost and he turned to McPherson.

"I must collect a few things in case the house is destroyed." Vinca and Syn joined them and the situation was explained.

"I'd rather not take the ship in," said McPherson gravely.

"Why not use a launch?" said Syn.

"Do that and I'll keep as close in as I dare but get back as soon as you can," said McPherson.

The launch was lowered and the three clambered in for the girls refused to remain behind. There was no danger involved for they could be there and back well within the time limit set by McPherson. The launch shot away at full speed leaving a creamy wake behind it. Vinca had taken the wheel and Triton lolled back with Syn. He glanced at her casually. She had not mentioned Antony's name since that awful day when she had received his letter. Her beautiful face was in repose and her golden hair streamed backward in the wind. She was in a reverie and looking at her again he could discern no sign of sadness in her face. Her sculptured features were a warm brown from the Caribbean sun and they looked somehow to him more mature, expressing a resoluteness and depth of character he had not noticed before. Feeling his glance upon her she looked at him with her calm green eyes and smiled warmly.

As they sped across the surface of the blue sea under a brilliant tropical sun, he thought how strange it was that their motive power was being generated in faraway misty Scotland.

Vinca, without slowing, made for the opening in the coral reef. She shot through it and crossing the lagoon at full speed drove the launch well up on the sandy shore. They were home again and with light hearts they leaped out on the sand. Four men suddenly materialized from the trees and stood silently covering them with automatic rifles. The girls gasped and turned to Triton who stood immobile at this unexpected welcome. Possible plans of action flashed through his mind. They could dive back into the sea in an attempt to escape. The gunmen however looked efficient and businesslike and might machine-gun them before they got away. Burchard appeared from the trees and walked down the sand as these thoughts passed through Triton's mind. Burchard stopped some distance away.

"Come up to the house," he said coldly and turning, retraced his steps.

There was not much they could do but obey and they followed, flanked on either side by the gunmen.

Triton realized his house had been taken over when they entered the living room. Burchard wasted no time on ceremony.

"Where's the diamond mine?" he asked coldly, looking at Triton steadily with his slaty eyes.

Triton could feel his cold detachment and realized

he would shoot them with as little emotion as he would destroy a fly. He was quite capable of killing one of the girls just to show he meant business, thought Triton, and felt fear begin to hammer in his chest. The girls stood white-faced and silent under cover of the guns.

"The mine is under water."

"We'd already deduced that," said Burchard curtly. He spoke to his men.

"Get the aqualungs." He turned to Triton. "You've no diving equipment in the house," he said suspiciously.

"It's on the ship," replied Triton quietly.

Vinca turned her head in surprise, but Burchard accepted the statement. Triton did not want him to know they were independent of such equipment. It might give them an opportunity to escape later and he prayed that neither of the girls would give the game away.

The men returned with the diving gear. Burchard considered the situation. He had sent one man in the boat to the other side of the island as soon as the schooner had been sighted, not wishing to give warning of his presence to anyone entering the lagoon. That left him with four men not including himself.

They had adequate diving equipment with plenty of cylinders, spare masks and breathing pieces, not knowing how long their search might last. He did not feel inclined to leave the girls in the house where there was a radiotelephone even if it was apparently without power. It was a slight risk but best avoided.

"Where do you get your power from?" he asked studying the two girls.

He realized he had never seen better-looking

dames, especially the cool blond one—and felt excitement begin to stir in him at the thought of disturbing her calmness.

Triton hesitated.

"It's broadcast."

Johnson, who had entered carrying a pair of cylinders, whistled at the remark. He was an educated man although he had been thrown out of Harvard before taking his degree.

"It would fit the situation but it's impossible," he said dumping the cylinders. He looked at Triton curiously.

"Where is it transmitted from?"

"Get these three fixed up first, we can go into all that later," said Burchard impatiently.

Burchard had decided to take all of them to the mine; it would be safer that way, he reasoned, and Averill would be less likely to try and play any tricks.

Bent slightly under the weight of their aqualungs the eight of them walked slowly down to the lagoon.

"You lead the way, Averill, and don't try any funny business or it will be the worse for you. We shall punish the girls if you attempt anything," he added with a nasty grin. He put his revolver in a protective waterproof case and each man armed himself with a harpoon gun. Burchard swam beside Triton, and the girls followed, each flanked by gunmen who would shoot if necessary.

Both Vinca and Syn hated the wretched aqualung which made them feel unwieldy in the sea. Triton led them to the cave and they climbed clumsily over the small beach onto the firm sand.

Burchard immediately removed the aqualungs

from his three captives, much to their relief—which would have astonished him if he had known it—and then freed his revolver. Not until then did he look round the well-illuminated cave.

"Where are the diamonds?" he asked harshly.

Triton pointed to the beach and Burchard looked with disbelief. With an excited cry he bent down, and began to pick them out while his men greedily began to do the same.

This was the moment Triton had waited for. He glanced at the girls and said one word: "Go!" Simultaneously they dived into the water.

As they disappeared beneath the surface Burchard fired but even as he did so realized it was useless. He was not, however, unduly worried for they could not get far without aqualungs. He congratulated himself on removing them. They would soon be caught and it would be an opportunity to get rid of Averill who was now of no further value.

"Roberts and Faber, go after them, they can't get far. Shoot Averill and bring the girls back here."

There were sniggers of approval and the two men pulled down their masks, waded into the water and sank below the surface leaving a trail of bubbles.

Burchard's bullet had by chance ricocheted and struck Syn on the temple. Its speed had been considerably diminished but the blow was severe enough to knock her out temporarily and as the two men submerged they collided with her. They surfaced and pushed her toward the beach; then resumed their underwater search for Vinca and Triton.

"Quick work," grinned one of the men on the beach looking up. Burchard grabbed and pulled her onto the sand. She lay on her back and the three of them admired her long-legged beauty which her bikini did little to hide. Two spots of color appeared on Burchard's sallow cheeks.

"She ain't breathing," said one.

"Why the hell kill a dame like that," growled the other angrily and they returned to their task.

Burchard put his hands on Syn's chest, felt her heart beating strongly and realized she was still alive. He looked at the two men busy collecting diamonds and one part of his calculating mind recognized that the present situation was explosive. Who could have anticipated wealth on such a scale—and so easily obtainable.

He looked at Syn lying defenseless and near naked at his feet and decided there was no need to share her until he had to.

"You realize we've nothing to carry the stones in," he said.

Johnson and Warner looked up at him blankly. They could pile them up but could not transport them.

"Go back to the house and get some bags, even pillowcases will do," he said.

The men got to their feet. What Burchard said made sense.

"Wait until I join you. In view of this we'll have to review our plans," he said waving his hand at the beach. The men grinned and waded into the sea. Burchard's gaze returned hungrily to Syn. Her color was still good and her heart beat strongly. Kneeling over her he started artificial respiration. He leaned backward and forward rhythmically driving the air needlessly in and out of the girl's lungs. He rested in due course and looked at her as she lay relaxed as if sleeping. She was a beautiful creature he thought as his hands wandered over her. He heard the water bubbling behind him and rose to his feet as Roberts and Faber returned.

"Where's the girl?" he snarled seeing them empty-handed. One of them lifted his mask.

"Not a sign of them anywhere."

Burchard swore.

"They're making for the launch, and if they get away we don't know what help they can bring. Get there as quickly as you can."

"Where's Johnson and Warner?" asked Roberts.

"They've returned to the house for some bags. Stay by the launch until I get there."

The men submerged quickly.

Burchard turned with a sigh of satisfaction. He had got rid of them all for the time being and could now devote his whole attention to the lovely doll lying at his feet.

chapter nine

TRITON AND VINCA dived deep and with a burst of speed rapidly left the cave behind. When they realized Syn was not with them they slowed expectantly but the blue haze behind remained empty. They called her name but only the voices of the dolphins answered and several came nosing forward to greet them and word soon passed through the length and breadth of the Caribbean that Triton was back with his two companions. The news caused great pleasure in his own herd especially to Tron, a descendant of Triton's childhood friend. Anxiously the two of them turned back toward the cave.

They must rescue Syn, but how? Triton racked his brains as they cautiously drifted back through the water. One thing was certain, they must keep out of sight of the men with their powerful harpoon guns. If their whereabouts remained unknown they might stand a chance of pulling something off. They must know what was happening at the cave, yet remain invisible. Triton spoke with the dolphins and they agreed to become his eyes. He warned them of the guns, for dolphins are friendly creatures, and keeping their distance they watched unseen. Sound travels far in the water and they reported what was happening to Triton without changing their positions, although he was well out of their sight, he and Vinca being hidden behind a coral reef.

The dolphin spies described the actions of the first two men who were obviously searching for them. If the men saw the dolphins who were immobile in their strategic positions, they took no notice, and if they heard the flutes and squeaks of Dolphinese it was only another sound in the sea which meant nothing to them.

The dolphins reported that two men had left the cave and were swimming toward the lagoon. There was silence for some time after that and Triton had to control the impulse to plunge back into the cave in an attempt to rescue Syn. There could be only one end to such a hasty and ill-considered action.

At last the dolphins spoke again. The two searchers had entered the cave and almost immediately come out again and were now swimming strongly toward the lagoon in the wake of the first two.

"Follow them," commanded Triton.

There was now only one man in the cave with Syn and he could be dealt with. The dolphins trailed the men and reported that all four were now ashore.

Triton looked at his watch and saw that time was passing all too swiftly. He spoke rapidly and urgently to Vinca and both of them sped toward the cave.

Johnson and Warner emerged first from the lagoon, looking like prehistoric beasts. As soon as they saw the launch Johnson realized it was the only escape route for Averill and the girl. He turned to his companion.

"You guard the boat while I get the bags."

Warner grunted and faded among the trees while Johnson hurried up to the house. He collected five pillowcases, cut off some curtain cord and proceeded to hurry back to the lagoon—not wishing to miss any of the fun. As he emerged from the trees Roberts and Faber were wading ashore.

"What are you doing?" he asked.

"Burchard told us to guard the launch," said Roberts.

"Why did he stay behind?"

They looked at each other suspiciously.

"Let's get back," said Johnson and turned to Warner.

"You stay here in case they return. You know what to do?"

The man hawked and spat on the sand.

"I know," he said.

Johnson and the other two submerged immediately and began swimming for the cave. They reached the place where it should be but the entrance evaded them. Boulders and coral outgrowths abounded and they entered several caves but not the one they were looking for.

Triton and Vinca entered the cave and Triton remained submerged while Vinca floated helplessly to the surface as if exhausted and half drowned. She called out feebly for help and Burchard, with revolver in hand, approached the water's edge.

"Where's Averill?" he asked.

Vinca, partially submerged, frantically clawed her way to the surface.

"Help!"

"Where's Averill?" asked Burchard implacably.

Vinca was near the beach but appeared too exhausted to reach it without help. She had counted on immediate help—not this interrogation, having entirely misjudged the character of her adversary. Her woman's wit came to the rescue.

"A shark got him," she sobbed and made feeble attempts to reach the beach.

It looked to Burchard as if she might not make it and he considered dispassionately whether to let her drown or not. She was young and good-looking, and there were five men on the island. It was this and not humanitarian considerations which prompted his action. He kneeled down and put out a hand which she seized.

Syn, who had recovered consciousness some minutes before and had heard the conversation rose smartly and placing a shapely foot on Burchard's rump pushed. With a yell of surprise he entered the water firing at Vinca as he did so. The noise vibrated loudly in the cave. Triton, who had been worried at the unaccountable delay, seized Burchard in a steely grip and found he had got hold of a tiger. The gun was lost in the struggle and it was only Triton's ability to remain under water for a long time that eventually won the day. Syn, quite recovered from her temporary knockout, retrieved her brassiere. Triton was wondering what to do with the half-drowned Burchard when Johnson and the other two men appeared and immediately stuck their harpoon guns against them, while Syn stood hesitantly on the sand.

"Stay where you are," said Johnson ominously, "or these two will get it."

Syn stood impotently by while Johnson dragged Burchard onto the shore and left him. He turned toward the water.

"Out you two come if you don't want to be shot," he snarled. Vinca and Triton climbed out followed by the two men still covering them with their harpoons.

Johnson tied their hands behind their backs with the curtain cord, and then did the same to Syn. Not until then did he turn and look at Burchard. The man was white and stirred feebly. He coughed and vomited up water while his three associates watched curiously, making no effort to help him. The same thought was in the minds of all. If Burchard died there would be one less to share the diamonds. Burchard, however, was tough and it was not long before he sat up and then climbed to his feet. He looked steadily at Johnson and the other two and knew exactly what they had been thinking.

"Sorry to disappoint you," he sneered and walking up to Triton slashed him viciously across the face.

"I'll make you pay for that little experience," he said conversationally. "You're expendable now. Would you like to know how you're going to die?"

Triton looked at him steadily but made no reply. The silence lengthened until it became unbearable. Both men looked each other in the face neither willing to drop his gaze first. The atmosphere became tense and electric and was suddenly broken by Burchard who viciously slashed Triton's other cheek with his open hand. He spoke as if they were chatting pleasantly round a tea table.

"I'm going to burn you at the stake, Averill. We'll use one of your coconut trees at the edge of the lagoon. I understand it is a prolonged and painful death and while you howl you can watch us enjoy your two little friends on the sand at your feet."

There were gasps of horror from Syn and Vinca.

"Take them ashore," said Burchard.

The men bent to pick up the aqualungs.

"Leave those, drag them along as they are, but don't spoil the show by drowning them."

The men laughed and the tension broke. As Burchard pulled on his aqualung he spoke to Roberts and Faber.

"You take Averill between you, Johnson and I will take the girls." He adjusted his mouthpiece, pulled on his mask and turning to Syn twisted his hand in her hair until he had a good grip and dragged her into the water. He towed her through the entrance into the sea. Johnson did the same with Vinca while the other two men each slipped their arms under Triton's and gripped hands behind his back. However fast he swam he could only tow them. Any struggles on the girls' part caused excruciating pain—as if their scalps were coming off. As soon as they entered the sea Triton gave the distress call of the dolphins and Vinca and Syn did the same. The men looked at them curiously and wondered what they were doing. The calls immediately activated every dolphin in the vicinity and the great mammals came hurtling through the water like live torpedoes to rescue their friends. The beaklike heads of the dolphins struck their captors with irresistible force. Johnson was caught between two of them and his chest caved in as if it were made of fragile glass. His blood stained the water with a deep red. The other two were killed instantly. Burchard was struck by two at the same time but at such an angle that he was spun round in the water without receiving a fatal blow.

"Swim," shouted Triton urgently, seeing the cloud of blood, for he knew only too well what would happen, and surrounded by dolphins they fled rapidly from the scene of combat. They normally swam with their arms close to their sides so their speed was in no way diminished because of their bound hands. Their maneuverability was reduced however for they were unable to use their hands as directional flippers.

Burchard rose to the surface, wondering what on earth had happened. Johnson was floating beside him in a cloud of blood and seeing the grotesque positions of Roberts and Faber, as well as the absence of any air bubbles he realized they were dead as well. The attack had ceased as suddenly as it had begun and he congratulated himself on escaping with nothing worse than bad bruises. He was considering whether to return to the cave or not when he was suddenly bumped violently. The water round him turned scarlet and he looked stupidly at the stump of his arm. Something seized him by the leg and his cry of fear turned into a gurgle as he was dragged helplessly beneath the surface.

Gray shapes worried and pulled him to and fro in a gradually expanding red cloud which hid everything from sight. When at last the bloodstained water cleared there was no sign of either men or sharks.

As soon as Triton considered they were a safe distance away he slowed and stopped. Syn and Vinca, who swam on either side of him, did likewise, automatically maintaining their position with mathematical precision as they did so. They had to free themselves as soon as possible and Triton was relying on the dolphins to do it. It was a terrible feeling to be tied and defenseless in the deep sea, where they would be an easy prey to the first hungry shark they met.

He had only to tell the dolphins what he wanted and these highly intelligent mammals who were his friends would cooperate and remove their bonds. He pondered how he would make his request in a language that possessed no word for rope, nor any way of expressing such a concept as "tied." He spoke carefully to Tron, the descendant of his old friend.

Triton was held in awe by the dolphins for two reasons. First they realized he was in the shape of a man in spite of living and belonging to a dolphin herd. Not only that, he enjoyed the position of a disseminator among dolphins—one who is a repository of knowledge and a teacher although Triton had never exercised the latter function. Nevertheless, he was one of them, both in language and behavior and had even made the long trek—an obligation of every full-grown male. This man-dolphin was held in high esteem by them all and the dolphin disseminators passed on this attitude to the younger generation. All dolphins scattered through the seas knew about him, though the majority would never see him. But wherever he went in dolphin country he traveled among friends who would obey him willingly and without question.

He spoke carefully to Tron.

"My hands are stuck together as strongly as a

mussel to a rock, and many close strands of seaweed hold them together. Can you bite through them, Tron?"

"I'll separate them," said the dolphin confidently. Triton spiraled down to the seabed and lay on his stomach so as to offer maximum resistance.

The dolphin followed and nosed his friend's hands, his powerful twelve-foot body standing almost vertical in the water. The lips of a dolphin are rigid and Tron found his beak-shaped head a disadvantage. With a few flicks of his tail he placed himself at right angles to the body below him so he could use the side of his mouth. Triton could not help wincing as he felt the strong jaws close gently on his hands, although he had implicit faith in Tron's ability and judgment. He had been brought up by dolphins since infancy and rated their intelligence as high if not higher than man's. Although an error of judgment on Tron's part could easily sever his hands Triton kept perfectly still as the calflike teeth behind the rigid lips attempted to sever his bonds. The dolphin tried repeatedly but could not get a grip on the cord.

"I cannot reach the strands," he said at last sadly.

"Shall I try with your knife?" asked Vinca.

Triton hesitated.

"Syn could watch and tell me how to move it," she added. In the upper air he would not have hesitated but it was dangerous to shed blood in the sea and if they tried to free themselves that way it would be almost unavoidable. He was also worried about time which must rapidly be running out.

"We'll swim to the ship," he said and spoke to Tron. "We shall need protectors."

"You shall have them," said Tron.

"Pass the warning that a mighty wave is coming and all dolphins who do not wish to be cast upon the land must swim well out to sea."

"It shall be done," said Tron and word was passed at speed through the sea from dolphin to dolphin until none remained near the coasts.

Captain McPherson was very worried. Triton and the two girls had been gone much longer than they intended and he feared something must have happened to them. The six hours were nearly up and anytime after that the tsunami could be expected.

If they were caught on or near the island they would almost certainly be killed. For the hundredth time he searched the sea with his binoculars. He dared not take the ship nearer to the island though he longed to do so in search of his friends. He stood anxiously on deck feeling impotent. He must wait here, however, so they would have a place of safety to which they could return. If he followed them to the island which every instinct in him screamed to do he would merely destroy the ship without helping them. As time had passed he had anxiously crept nearer to the island but as the danger hour approached he had been forced to retreat again to what he considered a safe distance. He lifted his binoculars again and this time saw a large number of dolphins approaching at speed. He held the glasses on them and realized they were making straight for him and swimming at a prodigious rate. He hoped and prayed Triton and the girls were with them. He glanced at his watch and saw the six hours were up. The herd were near now and he thought they were going to hit the ship but they split at the last moment, some passing under the prow and others under the stern. He looked eagerly and to his relief saw his friends surrounded by dolphins. Triton raised his head out of the water.

"Our hands are tied, send a man down to free us."

"Mr. Greenway," bellowed McPherson but Greenway had heard and was already running to the stern. He went down the rope ladder fast and cut Triton's bonds, who then took his clasp knife and freed the girls. They swarmed up the rope ladder.

"Thank heaven you're back, what the devil happened?"

"I'll tell you later—any sign of anything?"

"Not yet," said McPherson looking round the sea and sky. Everything appeared calm and quiet, unnaturally quiet.

"There's not a gull in sight," said McPherson. They leaned over the rail and gazed at Crab Island. An ominous silence seemed to descend and no one spoke. The ship was standing off a good way from the island but as they watched, it seemed to raise itself a little in the air while they gazed spellbound. A white line approached it from the sea and as it got nearer, Crab Island appeared to sink back again and the line of foam swept over it. Suddenly from the center of the island a column of what appeared to be thick white smoke jetted into the air, and the line of foam continued across the island to the other side.

Warner remained hidden among the palm trees where he could keep a close watch on the launch without being seen. As time passed and nothing happened he risked lighting a cigarette which he smoked carefully. What were the others doing in the cave, he wondered. The longer he waited the more suspicious he became. If their boat returned from the other side of the island where it had been hiding, it could pick up the men and the diamonds and leave him stranded here. He lit another cigarette, and cursed the heat. He smoked in nervous puffs and then dropped the butt. As he put his heel on it he listened. The island was suddenly quiet. The birds were silent and even the continuous cry of the gulls had ceased. He looked up at the sky which was an unmarred blue dome and walked nervously out from the trees onto the sand. He looked at the lagoon and along the sandy shore and all seemed normal except for the silence which was suddenly broken by strange sounds. He gazed stupidly at the sea which appeared to be retreating. It fell away down the sloped shores of the island, making queer gurgling and sucking sounds as it went. Patches of coral growths and rocks were suddenly exposed, while stranded fish flapped in agony on the suddenly naked seabed.

A peculiar stench assailed him and the sea slowly gathered itself together, rose and with a white foamy crest hurtled forward and upward with irresistible force. Warner screamed in terror and plunged inland through the trees but he could have stood still for all the difference it made. The high wave had crossed the lagoon almost before it started and foamed across the island, while everything went down before it. Trees vanished and the wall of water engulfed the house, destroying everything in its path. The suddenly increased pressure in the subterranean cave blew off the roof. A column of foaming water jetted high into the air, casting rocks across the island like a volcano and spewing the precious beach far and wide.

chapter ten

THE *Poseidon* kept well out to sea until the violence
was over and only when things had returned to
normal did she venture homeward. She crept into a
lagoon full of floating fish and all on deck gazed
upon a scene of devastation. The sandy shore was
littered with debris and broken tree trunks. They
picked their way with difficulty toward the house,
walking round obstacles and climbing over the
trunks of broken trees. They passed a large tiger
shark which gazed at them with unseeing eyes, its
body impaled on a broken branch. Sea Mount was a
ruin. The girls moved close to Triton each slipping
an arm through one of his. Their home, with all the
lovely things it contained, was gone, and they looked
upon it with sorrow. McPherson sympathized as they
stood there in silence and thought what a bitter blow
it must be to them. He would have been surprised if
he had experienced their emotions. They were true
children of the ocean where the concept of ownership does not exist as it is understood among men.
Property and ownership were concepts they had to

learn when they lived upon the land. Jealousy to possess and greed to retain were foreign emotions which they had to grasp intellectually in order to understand them.

Personal possessions they still tended to regard as objects passing through their hands rather than exclusively owned. They grieved at the destruction of their home and of something they considered beautiful but in a detached sort of way with a lack of emotional content which McPherson would have found strange.

They walked to the center of the island, curious about the column of smoke they had seen. As they approached the hole that had once been the roof of the cave they heard a loud hissing noise and observed the escape of vapors from the ground. They stood at the edge of the crater and looked down at the sandy floor. The noise appeared to come from beneath their feet and they circled the opening until they were looking at the raised lava floor. From where they stood the sun shone down, illuminating the smooth black rock and a crack in the wall behind it from which hissed a stream of gases.

"What is it?" asked Vinca puzzled.

"Either the earthquake has opened a geological fault, or the enormous water pressure that must have built up in the cave has split the wall," said McPherson.

"But where's it coming from?" she asked curiously.

"From far below the surface, Vinca. It's a vent for the deep internal pressures of the earth and it will hiss like that forever," said McPherson solemnly.

"It spoils our lovely cave," she said sadly.

"Except that it's no longer one," said Syn and looked at Triton to see if the same thought had passed through his mind.

Triton stood gazing down thoughtfully, his brown chiseled face expressionless.

"What sort of pressure do you think it has?" said Syn looking at McPherson.

He shrugged his shoulders.

"It could be anything. If you attempted to block it up, the pressure would probably rise until it blew," he said thinking that was what she had in mind.

Triton looked at her speculatively as she asked the question. They made their way back to the ship.

The West Indians who were members of their household were dismayed at the loss of their homes. They were allowed ashore to salvage any possessions they might find, but they had difficulty in even determining the site of their thatched houses. They were depressed and despondent on their return until Triton told them that he intended to rebuild. They immediately recovered their spirits and there was much whistling and laughter in the galley.

There was nothing now to keep the *Poseidon* at Crab Island. After lunch was over they set sail for New York, their next port of call.

Triton, Syn and Vinca retired to their private quarters where the girls enjoyed a liqueur. They were both eager to know Triton's plans.

"Are you going to rebuild the house?" asked Vinca eagerly.

"Crab Island is our home, Vinca," he answered. She nodded happily.

"What about the gas pressure?" asked Syn.

"I thought you probably had that in mind," he said smiling at her.

"It looks as if we may have solved the problem of power," he added in a tone of satisfaction.

"Perpetual free power," mused Syn.

"The disaster seems to have had its compensations," said Vinca. "I wonder what New York will be like?" she added inconsequently.

The ship docked up the Hudson River, the crew remaining on board while Triton and the girls took a suite at a luxury hotel.

Syn and Vinca explored the city's possibilities with their usual enthusiasm. John had an office here and it was not long before they had a host of acquaintances and admirers.

The fame of their diamond necklaces alone would have made them *persona grata* without the added attraction of an English baronet as a guardian. Syn and Vinca did not enter New York with the same naive wonder as in London. They were wiser and more experienced. They had learned their lessons much more rapidly than any upper-air girl could have. Living in an environment where a mistake could mean death had given them razor-edged minds. They could evaluate at great speed and were incapable of making the same mistake twice. The consequences of one error immediately led them to see a host of possible lesser ones so that their development was rapid in the extreme. Their emotional experiences in London had clarified their feelings. They were no longer in love with love and both realized they had yet to meet anyone whom they could admire as much as they did Triton.

They were now able to assess his qualities which

previously they had been unable to do. His physical appearance had always been pleasing but they had taken it for granted until they had seen the varied shapes of upper-air men. Triton treated them as equals, with kindness and consideration, but without sentimentality. He was cool and unflurried in danger. His decisions were just and uninfluenced by any form of selfish motivation. These qualities and others only became apparent to them against the general background of human behavior. They discussed the matter at length between themselves and decided that so far they had met no upper-air man who approached him in stature.

After they had moved into their hotel he asked them if they would like their own apartment.

Syn looked surprised.

"Good heavens, no."

"Why ever should we want to leave you?" asked Vinca innocently and Triton looked blank.

Both girls remained largely oblivious to matters beyond their immediate interests. Not so their guardian, who watched with apprehension the uneasy currents of world affairs. The day after they arrived in New York a frontier quarrel between China and India reached a climax. Russia was on the side of China and with her moral backing, Chinese forces again crossed the border into India. India cried out that she was being invaded while China blandly stated she was only reentering her own territory. World diplomats looked on bleakly, fearful of escalation. India had the sympathy of the West and in due course received help in the form of arms shipments. After a few days more important domestic issues took the Chinese-Indian problem off the front page, and public interest waned.

Della Watson had been relieved at Antony's decision to go to Germany. He would be in a better position to make an unbiased decision about his future, away from the charm and beauty of Syn. She readily admitted to herself that the Phelan sisters were two of the loveliest girls she had ever seen. She had been curious and John had told her all about them. There was no blood relationship and she wondered why John had not fallen in love with one of them himself. She could think of such things now without distress. He was much older of course, but only chronologically. Physically and mentally he was not much older than they were. What an extraordinary situation, unbelievable if she did not know it to be true.

John would be in a similar predicament with any normal girl as Antony was with Syn, except that their roles would be reversed. John would watch his wife growing older while he remained the same, an unpleasant experience for them both.

The obvious solution was for John to fall in love with Vinca or Syn; such a marriage would be totally suitable. She wondered why it had not happened. The more she thought about it the more incredible it seemed to her that it had not occurred under such circumstances. It would be easy enough to fall in love with either of these lovely creatures or even both.

The sweep of her thoughts halted suddenly. Perhaps that was the reason, that he was in love with both of them. If he married one he would feel disloyal to the other. Did they feel the same, she wondered. No, of course not, or Syn would never have fallen in love with Antony. But both girls were very young and must be inexperienced in human relationships. Emotionally they were still growing up and probably did not know yet how they really felt. This was yet another reason why Syn and Antony should not marry. She was unlikely to break her ties completely with John and later on might find she was in love with him and poor Antony would suffer. Della made up her mind to visit Antony and try to influence him against such a marriage.

Antony was feeling miserable and homesick and was delighted at the suggested visit. Della took the cross-Channel ferry to Calais and then proceeded by train to Frankfurt. Antony had a small apartment in the outskirts of the city and was glad to see her. After dinner while she was considering how to broach the subject he spoke to her rather sadly.

"We are no longer engaged, Mother!"

She muttered a trite phrase of condolence and a wave of relief swept over her. Such a marriage could not be successful she knew.

"I wrote to Syn giving her a choice between her old life or marriage to me!"

He fumbled in his pocket and produced a letter.

"Here's her answer," he said handing it to her.

"Can I read it?"

He nodded his head.

My dearest Antony,

Your letter offered me a cruel choice, my darling, and has been pulling me in two ever since I received it. Half of me wishes to marry you and live happily ever after, while the other half is horrified at the thought of never again seeing or living in the cool green ocean. If I could give you the ability to join me there—if you could experience its freedom and beauty and feel how the cares and troubles of the upper-air world are washed away in its peaceful depths you would never have presented me with such an impossible choice. Not only would I have to abandon my own world but it would also mean cutting myself off from Vinca and John, the only others of my kind in existence. I realize now our marriage would only last a short time before you began to grow old and, who knows, perhaps jealous and resentful if I did not do the same. There is no guarantee that I would grow old even if I never entered the sea again. It was your phrase "I am more than willing to take the risk involved" that eventually decided me. If I gave up everything I would still feel I was on trial until the end of your life. If I did not age as you did I would have failed you. Such a situation would be intolerable and make a happy marriage between us impossible. I enclose your lovely ring, my darling, and will often think of you when in my own world.

Your ever lovingly,

Syn

Della folded the letter slowly.

"She's a wise girl. That's exactly what would have happened."

"I suppose so," he muttered.

Della made no further comments. The matter was

settled satisfactorily as far as she was concerned and there was no more to be said. Time would heal Antony's hurt and in due course he would find another girl and be happy again.

Triton was anxious to rebuild his house and restock the island as soon as possible and he required the assistance of an architect, builders, engineers and a horticulturist. He was anxious to make his island home self-contained and independent of the outside world, and did not mind what it cost to do so. He had not met mankind until he was an adult and he had the unbiased viewpoint of an alien. He had never been conditioned through a lengthy childhood to accept things as a matter of course. The critical faculties of his mind as regards codes of behavior had not been rubbed blunt by familiarity or public condonement and he observed the behavior of his own kind with a certain horror. Man's behavior appeared to him irrational. His continuous bloody wars that now involved the death of innocent nonparticipants appalled him. Though both sides always deprecated the deaths of innocent women and children, the slaughter would continue unabated. John's business experience opened his eyes to the internal pressures of greed and envy and a type of ruthlessness he could not have imagined. His recent experiences with Burchard were unfortunate and did nothing to change his pessimistic view. The dichotomy of man shook him and he could not understand his ability to hold two drastically opposed views at the same time. Men loved their own children yet could approve measures that inevitably destroyed others. John was a great reader of history and noticed the treatment of man by man. He marveled at the good-living, sober, religious citizens of Bristol who had made fortunes in the slave trade. The historical accounts of the Second World War made him believe that the majority of mankind must suffer from some kind of mental illness and when he read about the atom bomb he was convinced man would eventually destroy himself. The great difference between him and other men was his immortality and if a day of reckoning came and there was a holocaust he and the two girls might well be the only ones left.

He did not wish to see the beauty of Vinca and Syn marred by the violence of men or their lovely bodies withering away from starvation or radiation poisoning.

He decided to prepare Sea Mount as a refuge and set about the task to the best of his ability. There was a tremendous lot of work for him to do and he went at it with all possible speed. The name of Sir John Averill was well known and he quickly obtained appointments with the men at the top who listened carefully to what he had to say.

He spent a long session with one of the most famous architects in New York, who agreed to design his new house. Crab Island had twice been attacked and Triton determined to build a more formidable residence this time that could not be entered so easily. The architect was surprised at his requirements but proceeded along the lines requested.

His next appointment was with a famous engineering firm which specialized in high-pressure equipment. He explained what he wanted and Raeder, an expert in the field, left shortly for Crab Island.

Syn and Vinca continued their studies and Syn was by now a very good mechanic with a widening insight into power mechanisms, while Vinca was rapidly becoming an expert marine biologist. They did not let this interfere with their pleasures, however, and with a rapidly growing group of friends and admirers they enjoyed all the delights New York had to offer. Both Syn and Vinca were subjected to high-pressure admiration by the American male. In the play of human relationship they were something apart, and the feelings they engendered in others made them even more fascinating. These three who had almost been born and bred in the sea, to whom the wide ocean and not the land was home, had never received any human conditioning. From infancy all children are brainwashed, emotionally, politically and religiously and it is this varied conditioning which makes mutual understanding so difficult. As a consequence of this every human being has certain sensitized areas of thought or belief. When these are touched upon adversely there is an automatic emotional reaction with its complex chemical response. Adrenalin is poured into the blood stream and the situation can no longer be met on a cool intellectual level. However intelligent a man may be he possesses these weaknesses of reflex emotional response which prevent a full understanding of another human creature.

The fascination these three exerted on those who met them was no doubt partly due to the absence of such conditioning. They had never been brainwashed by parents or relations, by church or chapel, by local customs or public opinion. As a consequence they possessed no sensitized areas capable of triggering an aggressive emotional reaction. And they were unique in this respect.

Triton was anxious to go to London where Dr. Noyes' work on his new computer was drawing to a successful conclusion. He wished to move his broadcasting equipment to Crab Island now he thought the question of power had been solved, and was only waiting for expert corroboration that this was so.

Triton hoped, as Syn had done, that the pressure from the underground leak that hissed incessantly into the cave could be controlled to drive a turbine and so generate electric power. He was anxious to possess a permanent power supply so that he could be independent of the outside world.

Raeder eventually returned from Crab Island and the two men met. Triton was shown into the president's office. He was no ordinary client and was treated with the respect due to the chairman of Electronic Equipment Ltd., a firm that was even bigger than their own.

Raeder had been chosen for the job because of his highly successful work in their North Sea gas undertaking. He was an expert in this particular type of work and the problem Averill had presented them with seemed one that called for his particular talents.

He was a short stocky man with a shock of black hair, and he looked at Sir John Averill curiously. He had been astonished at the remoteness of Crab Island and could not conceive why anyone should wish to go to the expense of building a power plant in such an isolated spot. He knew there was no industry or any other call for power in that vicinity for he had made it his business to find out. That only left the possibility of a local power supply for a private house, the equipment for which could easily be purchased without his expensive trip. After his survey of the island however, he thought he knew what must be in Sir John's mind, though why he could not be frank about it he could not imagine. The possibility of commercial exploitation he considered doubtful because of the distance involved, and the depth of the sea. As they took their seats he decided to let Averill do the talking.

"Is the pressure from that leak sufficient to drive a turbine and produce electricity?" asked John.

"How many volts do you wish to generate?"

"At least thirty-three thousand."

"But that's sufficient for industrial use," said Raeder in surprise.

"I know that."

Raeder kept silent out of sheer surprise. Why would Averill want so much power in that out-of-the-way spot, he wondered.

"Well?" said Triton sharply.

"I couldn't guarantee to do that," said Raeder and watching Averill he saw a look of disappointment cross his face.

He does not know, thought Raeder to himself. He is only interested in producing power, though heaven knows why.

"You can produce as much power as you like on the island, though not by pressure."

John looked up eagerly.

"How then?" he asked.

"That leak taps a field below the seabed of inflammable gas with a high carbon monoxide content." He paused.

157

"Go on," said John.

"With adequate heat, and you've certainly got that, we can build a conventional power unit producing steam to drive the turbine and generator."

Triton felt a deep satisfaction for at last he had a power source. It was the one thing he had feared might prove impossible.

"Can you say how long the gas will last?"

Raeder smiled.

"With only you using it, I'd say forever."

It was just the answer Triton wanted.

"I want you to build me such a power plant as soon as you possibly can," he said, and left Raeder with a puzzle that he never solved.

chapter eleven

AS SOON AS Triton had made his arrangements and set all the necessary wheels in motion he flew to London. The three of them would be staying with Raynor who was looking forward to their visit. Before their arrival, however, he had a sudden relapse and died.

They were in time to attend his funeral—Triton sad and grieving at the loss of his old friend and the girls wide-eyed and subdued at their first encounter with the rites of upper-air death. During the service Triton thought nostalgically of the kind little man who had been Oswald Raynor. He remembered their first meeting on the original *Poseidon,* the research ship from which he had been ignominiously hauled out of the sea in the nylon trawl. Oswald had helped him find Della, and meticulously handled his financial affairs when he had been incapable of doing so himself. He suddenly realized how much he owed his old and first friend and felt a deep sense of loss.

The service was well attended for Oswald had been an important man in the City and was widely liked. Triton caught a glimpse of the huge bulk of Rodique, one of the diamond merchants who had been present at the meeting arranged by Raynor in Hatton Garden, but the only person there he knew well was Dr. Crane who had been the biologist on the research ship. Oswald Raynor and Jack Crane had been two of his greatest friends and he was pleased and thankful to see Jack. They shook hands silently with no need for words, each knowing how the other felt.

"Come back to the house with us," said Triton. Jack nodded, and the four of them drove back sadly to Eaton Square.

Oswald Raynor had left no dependents, and had divided his estate between his two friends. He had left a substantial income for life to Jack Crane and the remainder, including his interests in Raynor and Reynolds, the merchant bankers, to his dear friend John Averill. This involved John in a considerable amount of work and it was some time before he could attend to his other affairs.

When at last he was free he paid his long-promised visit to Dr. Noyes and was shown the new computer. He was astonished at its size. It was a plain metal box six feet by four connected with what appeared to be a typewriter. Triton touched the keys.

"Is this a part of it?" he asked.

"It's your method of communication. You type your question and the computer answers in the same way. You can plug in three typewriters and use them at the same time."

"Can you give me a demonstration?"

Dr. Noyes shook his head.

160

"It's a moron at the moment, with no memory."

"I see," said Triton thoughtfully and wondered if it would take all he wanted to put into it. "It's very small," he added.

"Of course, its the ultimate in miniaturization." Noyes tapped the metal surface proudly. "There is no clumsy mechanical equipment in here. You are utilizing the basic building units of matter itself." He looked up with a smile. "Electrons are too small to be seen and the capacity of their memory bank is infinite."

Triton had subsidized Dr. Noyes in his work because it was a brilliant new conception which if successful would revolutionize the computer industry.

One of the difficulties with regard to modern computers was memory storage. He looked at the small metal box speculatively. Here, if Dr. Noyes was correct, was the answer to that problem. Triton believed that one day man would go to the stars if he did not destroy himself first. If that day ever came he might well live to see it. Conditions on earth might then make the settling of a new world an enviable goal. He had decided to fill the computer with all the knowledge that would be vital in such an enterprise. The taming of a new world would require all the skills which had been acquired so slowly and laboriously by the human race. Here was a way to store and transmit such information. He explained to Dr. Noyes what he wanted.

"That will take some programing," the scientist said pursing his lips.

"I want it done as soon as possible. Get the best

man you can in each specialty and remember that in a job like this money does not count."

This necessary piece of his plan taken care of, John and the two girls drove to Scotland where they stayed with Dr. Cunningham and his wife. They made a leisurely journey, admiring the scenery and staying at ancient inns on the way, so that it was a good ten days before they reached their destination.

They received a warm welcome and both girls immediately asked to see the broadcasting machine. Syn was especially keen but Dr. Cunningham already knew how interested she was.

They looked at the slick stainless-steel casing of the machine that disseminated the power which drove their ship across distant oceans. Vinca, seeing it for the first time, remembered how it had sent their launch on that ill-fated sultry afternoon across the lagoon into the menacing guns of the diamond thieves. It was purring steadily and Syn, putting her hand on it, could just discern a faint and steady vibration.

She looked at Triton.

"It's lovely," she said and with those two words won the heart of Dr. Cunningham.

For the next month he taught them all he could about this unique machine, the only one of its kind in the world.

It was dismantled and reassembled, and its scientific principles minutely explained. Each took it down in turn and reassembled it, and was grilled exhaustively by Cunningham afterward, until he was satisfied that it would be adequately maintained, even if they did not fully understand it.

When the three of them returned to London the plans and drawings of Sea Mount were waiting and Triton showed them to the girls.

"It's nothing like the old house," exclaimed Vinca excitedly.

"It's much bigger," said Syn examining the plans carefully.

"And difficult to break into," added Triton.

"What are the two wings for?" asked Syn.

"One is for the staff, who will not be separated from us this time. The other is for machinery." He placed a finger on the plan. "Here we'll house the electric generator, the broadcast machine and our new computer."

They looked at him in surprise for it was the first time they had heard about it.

"What's a computer for?" asked Vinca curiously.

"It is a machine which will contain most of the knowledge of the human race," said Triton remembering uneasily its small size.

"How do you use it?" said Syn eagerly.

"That reminds me, both of you must learn to type."

They looked mystified.

"That is how you will communicate. You type your question and the machine answers in the same way."

"How amazing," said Vinca. "Will it answer any question?"

"I hope so," said Triton gravely.

They returned to London and the girls immediately joined type-writing classes where they worked hard until both became efficient typists.

Between times they shopped and the girls spent

delirious hours choosing curtains and carpets. They had a large establishment to furnish and they spent months carefully selecting and choosing what they wanted. Triton made it clear that cost was no consideration so they bought according to taste and requirement, unhampered by any financial restriction.

Meanwhile the *Poseidon* remained in her berth up the Hudson so that McPherson could stay with relatives outside New York.

Syn and Vinca had innate good taste and they bought wisely and well, calling in Triton only at the last moment in case he disagreed with their choice. They bought Persian carpets, curtains, furniture, silver, linen, crystal, pictures and objets d'art. Triton spent hours choosing books for the library, chiefly autobiographies, histories, travel books and novels, since all technical knowledge would be in the computer. Syn however could not resist books on engineering, while Vinca added generously to her library on zoology and purchased a lot of laboratory equipment as well.

These purchases were packed and held ready for transport. The broadcasting machine, when they were ready for it, would be crated and brought down by a special truck with Dr. Cunningham, who insisted on traveling with it. All they waited for now was the arrival of the ship which was due in the next few days, and the computer.

The *Poseidon* duly arrived from New York and went to her old berth in Quebec Dock. Captain McPherson phoned Triton and was invited to stay at Eaton Square.

Holds number two and three amidships had been

cleared for their purchases, and the crew were given leave in turn, two always remaining on board.

They drew lots and Nero and Avon remained during the first week. Their duties were light and they had no reason to be on their guard so they failed to notice the ship was under constant but discreet surveillance.

Triton and the girls had felt the call of the sea for a considerable time now. They could not remain away from it long without the irresistible impulse to return mounting until it became a desire they could not withstand. It would not be long now before their return to the Caribbean and they decided on the spur of the moment to visit the *Poseidon* which was their link with home. They drove down and leaving the Rolls on the quayside walked aboard. They called out but there was no cheery response from the crew.

"That's funny, where's everybody?" said Triton.

They walked toward the main cabin, the door opening at their approach. The entire ship was electrified and possessed a vast number of gadgets, many of them under Triton's direct control.

As she was able to draw unlimited power from the air there was no need to economize and all doors had photoelectric eyes and slid open when approached and closed again afterward. The three of them walked in unsuspectingly, heard the door close and found themselves covered by guns. Nero and Avon, trussed and gagged, lay in a corner while three gunmen sat facing the door. They rose as Triton entered, each one aiming his weapon steadily. Two remained facing them while the other slipped between them and the door.

The tallest looked at Triton and spoke in a cold voice. "Come over here if you don't want to be shot."

Triton noticed as he walked toward him that his weapon was fitted with a silencer. He looked at Nero and Avon, hoping they had not been harmed. They gazed at him with complete confidence and he smiled grimly, guessing their thoughts. As the merman of the Caribbean he would be expected to deal out justice, probably with just a wave of his hand, he thought wryly. He was now facing the gunman.

"Turn round and put your hands behind you."

He did so and a pair of handcuffs were snapped immediately round his wrists.

"You girls stand beside him," said the man pointing with his gun, and while two kept them covered the third man slipped out of the room.

"What do you want?" asked Triton but they watched him impassively without replying.

After a long wait in strained silence heavy footsteps approached the door which opened obediently to admit Rodique followed by the third gunman.

"That's rather neat," said Rodique watching the door as it slid shut behind him. He turned and calmly looked the two girls over, ignoring Triton.

"Very attractive," he murmured appreciatively. Triton watched him coldly. Raynor's surmise had been correct, he thought. This hulk of a man was the cause of all their troubles. Rodique looked round the cabin whose portholes on one side showed a view of the quay.

"We can't operate here or we shall be heard," he said.

"There are two empty holds down below," answered one of the men.

"Excellent, let us proceed there immediately."

The three of them were roughly herded down into number three hold, which was empty.

Rodique looked at one girl, then the other and pointing to Syn spoke sharply.

"Strip her."

Nothing loath, two of them approached with salacious grins and seized Syn. But instead of a frightened defenseless young girl they found they had hold of a jungle cat. Vinca sprang to her sister's aid and with a curse Rodique grabbed her. He stood holding her in his huge arms where she struggled impotently. Syn as not giving in lightly and the three men had their hands full. Triton sat watching, apparently unmoved. The most he could do would be to stand up and kick Rodique. It might temporarily release Vinca who would join in the fray again, but it would only mean that both girls would get hurt more than if he left things as they were. He controlled himself, holding in his anger in a way the deep sea had taught him. Syn had marked the faces of all three men, and they were cursing as blood dripped from their chins. Rodique looked on amused and Vinca gave up her useless struggles. The men at last let Syn go and she stood at bay, straight and slim. Rodique dropped Vinca who, taken by surprise, fell to the floor.

"Get her," he said and as they grabbed Vinca he casually removed a leather crop from under his coat. He looked Syn over calmly and spoke to Triton for the first time as he slowly approached her, his crop at the ready. She retreated slowly while the three men stood out of the way with their backs to the wall, with Vinca held firmly between them.

Rodique suddenly lashed out and although Syn tried to jump out of the way she was struck across the shoulder and a red weal appeared on her skin.

"I sent men to find your diamond mine—lash—but they disappeared—lash—I want to know—lash—where it is."

He followed Syn deliberately as she slowly retreated. She watched him calmly and turned and twisted to avoid his blows but the room was too small and for every blow she dodged she received two.

"When I've killed this girl—lash—I'll start on the other."

His efforts began to make Rodique grunt. Otherwise there was silence in the room.

"I'll tell you," said Triton reluctantly.

"Where is it?" he said still following Syn.

"On Crab Island, but you'd never find it."

Rodique paused and looked at him for the first time.

"I knew it," he said triumphantly.

"Give me a pen and paper," said Triton resignedly.

"Free him but keep him covered," said Rodique for he remembered that six tough men had disappeared trying to find out the secret.

Triton rubbed his wrists and sneezed. He could override the electric controls of the ship with a small gadget which was in his trouser pocket. He sneezed again and replaced his handkerchief.

"We'll take you upstairs, Averill, and leave your

two little friends here to make sure you play no tricks."

Triton manipulated the device and locked every door in the ship. He opened the seacocks and water began to pour into the bilge below the floor, and it came in fast for the hold was well below water.

"What's that," exclaimed Rodique hearing the noise. Triton rose lazily.

"The seacocks are open, let's go," he said.

Rodique approached the door which of course did not open. At the same time water began to creep over the floor. Rodique banged and pushed without result.

"How do you open the damn thing?" he said turning angrily.

"It's automatic, the water must have short-circuited it," said Triton calmly.

It was now swirling over their ankles and rising rapidly. One of the men rushed at the bulkhead door to beat on it frenziedly and then emptied his gun at it without effect. Ricocheting bullets clanged and reverberated deafeningly, to say nothing of the danger to them all.

"We'll be drowned like rats," the wretched man gabbled. Rodique struck him savagely across the face.

"Shut up," he snarled. He heaved on the slide door, trying to push sideways, but it was immovable. There were small beads of sweat on his pasty face as he turned to Triton.

"This is some trick of yours," he snarled.

"I don't wish to drown any more than you do. The door can be opened from the outside easily enough. Try and attract the crew."

The water was now creeping up to their knees and one man began muttering hysterically. The other two beat on the door with their fists, their guns dropped and forgotten in their panic. The water reached their waists and continued to rise. Rodique's fat face was trembling and his left eyelid twitched. Triton regarded him calmly.

"If you had not tied up my crew they could have opened the door by now. I fear you are going to drown, Rodique; you've signed your own death warrant."

The water was now up to the big man's chest.

"So will you," he gasped.

"We shan't, Rodique, but you will," said Triton evenly. Rodique's eyes opened wide and then he was floundering about with the other three, and their cries of fear vibrated in the small air space left. The two girls swam to Triton and inhaling deeply the three submerged. The air was displaced through the deck above and the thrashing bodies slowly became still. Triton manipulated the gadget and started the pumps. They waited calmly while the water level slowly dropped. Triton examined Syn's bruises when it reached their waists, for the fluorescent lights had remained alight throughout.

"You're a very brave girl," he said gently.

She gave him a trembling little smile and putting her arms round his neck hid her face against his chest.

Vinca pushed one of the floating bodies away distastefully with her foot.

"They were wicked men," she said, "and I'm glad they're dead."

When the hold was almost empty Triton opened the door.

"See to the crew, Vinca, while I tend to Syn."

Vinca hurried away, and Triton escorted Syn to their quarters. He dressed her back, and helped her into some loose clothes.

"Would you like to lie down?" he asked.

She shook her head and laughed.

"I think I'll be more comfortable standing."

He took her arm and they returned to the main cabin. Vinca had released Nero and Avon who were unhurt and was telling them what had happened. She stopped as Triton and Syn entered.

"Are you boys all right?" asked Triton.

"Yes, sir," they said in unison bending their heads slightly as they spoke.

Triton spoke carefully.

"If we report this there will be a prolonged investigation which may delay us indefinitely. These men caused us considerable inconvenience when they were alive, and I see no reason why they should continue to do so now they are dead."

He paused while they looked at him in silence.

"Miss Phelan is in no condition to travel so we shall sleep here. During the night I will tow our friends out into the river and set them adrift. When they are discovered there will be no connection with us, and we may be well out to sea before they are found."

Vinca, although she tried to hide it, was very upset at her sister's experience. She was most solicitous of her during the remainder of the day, repeatedly asking if she was comfortable, and producing cushions and a hassock on which Syn could rest

171

her feet. When they retired for the night she insisted on dressing Syn's bruises herself which she did with great tenderness, and then putting her arms around her she wept.

"I wish it had been me," she sobbed and Syn had to comfort her.

Triton was awakened by a gentle tapping.

"Who is it?"

The door opened quietly and Nero poked in his head.

"It's two o'clock, sir."

"I'll be with you in a minute."

The head withdrew and Triton put on his underwater accouterments and went up on deck.

Nero and Avon were standing in the stern, and he could hardly see them in the darkness. There was no moonlight and even the stars were obscured by cloud.

"We'll slide them down to you, sir," whispered Avon. Triton descended the rope ladder that was hanging over the stern and entered the water. Avon followed him but stopped halfway down while Nero slid one of the bodies over the side. Holding it by the feet he let it down until Avon grasped it and let it slip silently into the water.

Triton took his bearings, and seizing the corpse by the foot, submerged. He towed it underwater into the adjacent dock, and from there into the river where he let it go.

While he was doing this Avon and Nero brought another body on deck and were ready and waiting for him when he returned. Everything went well until they attempted to move Rodique whom they had left until last. He was a huge man and difficult

172

to move. It took their combined efforts to heave him onto the rail. Avon then descended the ladder while Nero attempted to lower him as he had the others. The man's weight, however, proved too much, and instead of sliding down gently he fell, striking Avon and wrenching his grip from the ladder so they both fell into the dock with a terrific splash.

Triton immediately seized the body and submerged while Avon with a few strokes grabbed the ladder and remained motionless in the darkness listening. All he could hear was the slap of water against the hull as the ripples of their fall slowly subsided. At this moment the moon showed its face through the clouds and the dock was illuminated by a silvery light, as if heaven were momentarily curious, but it soon faded as the clouds covered the moon again. All remained quiet and no cry or challenge disturbed the peace of the dock.

Avon crossed himself and as silently as a cat he ran up the ladder and regained the deck. Meanwhile Triton was holding Rodique down in the dark waters of the dock, but his hurried submergence had confused his sense of direction. He was forced to surface again in order to orient himself, but as his head broke water he was reassured by the silence. Although there was no direct moonlight there was a faint luminosity from the cloud layer sufficient for him to take his bearings.

The *Poseidon* loomed above him and he could just pick out the swing bridge under which he had to go. He submerged again and towing what had been Rodique through Canada Dock he entered the river and pushed him into the current. He returned silently to the ship, took a hot bath to wash off the oil and dirt and returned satisfied to his bed.

The next morning they drove to London and arranged for their purchases to be delivered to the ship and McPherson returned ready to receive them. Although the floor of number three hold had almost dried out McPherson spotted it at once and wanted to know what had happened. He questioned Avon and Nero who would say nothing but referred him to their master. Considerably annoyed, McPherson examined the hold carefully and looked at the seacocks. Everything was in order and, satisfied, he continued with his work, making a mental note to question Triton when he came aboard.

Crates began to arrive and McPherson supervised their storage in the holds. If this was not done skillfully they could shift during the voyage and cause havoc. Dr. Cunningham shut down the power plant, disconnected the broadcasting machine and personally supervised its packing. He traveled down in the truck with it and two duplicate machines, while his wife, excited at the thought of their trip to the Caribbean, traveled by train. She had only met Sir John Averill once or twice and thought it very kind of him to offer them such a lovely holiday.

Syn's resilient youth soon threw off the effects of the beating and by the time they were ready to sail the marks on her skin were beginning to fade. She looked forward to their return home and longed for her natural habitat, the warm shallows and coral reefs of the Caribbean sea.

Their days in London were now numbered and Triton had arranged to take Vicky out to a farewell dinner. The Duchess of Beaux had been delighted at

Triton's return to London, but she was desolated to learn that they were leaving—and without any immediate prospect of return, since John was deliberately vague on this point.

Living as one of the family for so long had enabled her to know Triton well and she realized that she would never meet anyone else who could mean so much to her as he did. She was looking forward with a mixture of pleasure and pain to the coming evening.

The two or three days following Syn's ordeal Triton and the girls had spent quietly at home. Triton looked at the clock and rose.

"I shan't be in to dinner," he said.

Both girls felt a sense of disappointment.

"Where are you going?" asked Vinca inquisitively.

"I'm taking Vicky out."

There was an icy silence, and he looked at them curiously.

"You aren't taking us out?" said Vinca accusingly.

"Syn hasn't felt much like it, have you Syn?"

She looked at him, her cheeks slightly flushed.

"You haven't asked me," she said tartly.

Triton was nonplused and felt himself being maneuvered into a potition of guilt, which was ridiculous. He spoke sharply.

"I'm looking foreward to a delightful evening with a very pleasant person."

"Who only thinks of one thing," added Syn smoothly.

"Such as?"

"He's still a child in these matters," said Vinca to her sister.

"What are you two young idiots talking about?"

"The last defense of the male—abuse," said Syn pityingly.

Triton flushed.

"Say outright what you mean and don't hedge like these humans," he demanded.

"Vicky has only one thought in her mind with regard to you," said Syn softly.

"She wants to marry you," blurted out Vinca.

Triton was taken aback at this outburst and looked at them with a sudden deeper understanding.

"Vicky unfortunately is an upper-air girl."

"Unfortunately indeed," sniffed Vinca.

Triton continued as if he had not heard.

"I have realized for a long time the impossibility of marrying upper-air creatures, who crumble and disintegrate so quickly. It would only bring unhappiness. They would be jealous of our youth, and we would be sad to see our loved ones become old and senile."

The girls' demeanor slowly changed as he spoke.

"Vicky is a lovely person really," said Vinca.

"One of the nicest of the humans," added Syn.

"I'm glad to hear you say so," he murmured as he walked to the door.

They darted out in front of him, produced his hat and gloves and helped him solicitously into his coat.

"Have a good time," said Syn kissing him lightly.

"Enjoy yourself and give Vicky our love," said Vinca, and saluted him in the same way.

Triton could not help smiling as he shut the front door behind him.

McPherson was fully occupied until the moment

the ship was ready to sail, so that it was not until they were well on their way that he remembered to ask Triton the reason for the damp floor in number three hold.

"I withheld the information on purpose," said Triton.

McPherson looked at him questioningly.

"Why?" he asked bluntly.

"As captain of the ship I was not sure how you would react or where your duty might be and decided to avoid presenting you with a possible dilemma."

He told him the whole story and McPherson listened in silence.

"So Raynor was correct in assuming it was Rodique," he said musingly.

"Without a doubt."

"Oswald was a smart man," said McPherson.

Triton nodded his head silently as he thought of his friend and all that he owed him and felt the pain of his loss afresh.

"It was a fitting end for a swine like Rodique and I'm glad your troubles are now over," said McPherson and neither of them referred to the matter again.

chapter twelve

∾⌇∾⌇∾⌇∾

THE *Poseidon* slipped down the Thames while Triton, Syn and Vinca stood in the bows. They leant over the rail watching the busy river traffic. Captain McPherson, contentedly smoking a cheroot, was in the wheelhouse with the pilot. Neither Triton nor the girls knew that this would be the last time they would see these sights and that never again would the *Poseidon* ride this great river.

All their purchases were safely stowed in the holds, including the broadcasting machine with two duplicates and a large collection of spares. Dr. Cunningham would install it personally on the island and both he and his wife were looking forward to the trip. With the broadcasting machine out of action the ship was without any electricity with which to cook or light, let alone to heat water and drive the engines. A temporary domestic power unit had been installed just for the journey to Crab Island. On arrival Dr. Cunningham would install the transmitter and the ship with her multiplicity of electric devices would again have her own power.

The computer was also aboard but it so fascinated the girls that it was kept in their private quarters. Dr. Noyes had taught them how to use it and they were continually asking it questions. Its colossal memory was divided into numerous sectors. If an engineering question was to be asked it was first necessary to be put through to Engineering Department. If this request was not typed first and an engineering question was asked of the Zoology Department the machine would type "Question not understood." There was a list of over five hundred departments which embraced all the skills of men. The information was comprehensive on every subject ranging from early primitive methods to the latest sophisticated techniques.

The Cunninghams were sunning themselves on deck as they crossed the bay. The ship was traveling fast before a brisk wind and the white-capped waves reflected back the strong sunlight. They were carefully ensconced in a protected corner where they faced the stern of the ship. Mrs. Cunningham, who had never been on a sailing ship before, stared up at the rigging and listened to the gentle thrumming of the wind and thought how exhilarating it all was, like riding a living creature. She would never choose a steamship in preference to this she thought as she gazed sternward. Her husband returned from his cabin with a book and looked anxiously at his wife.

"What's the matter, my dear?"

Mrs. Cunningham was a sensible Scotswoman, a very down-to-earth sort of person who was not given to fancies. She swallowed before answering, almost ashamed of what she was about to say, and looked searchingly at their foaming wake.

"I must be seeing things," she said.

The doctor sat in his deck chair and pulled a rug around him.

"What sort of things?" he asked.

"Sir John and those two charming girls have just dived overboard."

"What?"

"Keep your voice down," she said unnecessarily.

"What did you say?"

"Our host and his two wards have just dived over the stern."

He looked at the white-capped sea, observed the speed at which the ship was cleaving through the water and watched the turbulent white wake she was leaving behind her.

"Do you mean they have committed suicide?" he whispered.

"It didn't look like it, they had on some sort of swimsuits."

He looked at her closely but except for looking rather pale she appeared her normal self.

"Surely it's impossible," he said.

"I've just seen them, a moment before you returned." He looked round the ship. Captain McPherson stood imperturbably at the wheel smoking his inevitable cheroot.

"Did he see them?" he asked indicating the captain.

"He must be blind if he didn't. They ran past him and swallow-dived off the rail."

"His back would be toward them."

"He must have seen how they were dressed," she said sharply.

There was an awkward silence.

"Aren't you going to do anything?" she hissed.

"Perhaps I should speak to the captain."

"Do it then."

Cunningham rose reluctantly and strolled toward the poop deck. It was an embarrassing situation and he wondered how to broach the subject. He could hardly ask bluntly if his host had jumped overboard with his two wards. The captain would think him crazy. Captain McPherson watched him expectantly. He had observed with some amusement Mrs. Cunningham's horrified gaze and the earnest conversation with her husband on his return.

"Good morning, Dr. Cunningham."

"Good morning, Captain."

"It's a perfect day for sailing."

Dr. Cunningham nodded his head absentmindedly.

"Where's Sir John?" he asked bluntly.

Captain McPherson grinned.

"He's gone for a swim," he said in a matter-of-fact voice.

Cunningham's mouth dropped open as he looked at the racing sea.

"They'll be back for lunch," said the captain reassuringly.

Slightly stunned, Cunningham walked to the stern and looked over. The sea appeared to rush backward at great speed continually snatching and tugging at the swinging rope ladder that trailed in the water.

He returned to his wife and repeated the conversation. They sat there patiently for the remainder of the morning, their attention never distracted for long from the stern of the ship. Shortly before lunch they watched unbelievingly as Triton and the two girls

181

climbed casually over the rail and made for their cabins.

The wind remained favorable and they made good time across the Atlantic. In perfect weather they approached the West Indies, those scattered islands which lay like an ill-defined horseshoe between the Atlantic and the Caribbean. Triton and the girls stood in the prow waiting for their first glimpse of home. The ship seemed to share their emotion and plunged forward, hissing eagerly through the sea. At last a faint smudge appeared on the horizon, and in a short while Crab Island lay before them, a small green gem set in an azure-blue sea. They passed through the opening in the coral reef and the anchor dropped through the clear water of the lagoon. The Cunninghams, watching from the poop deck, thought it had the beauty of enchantment.

The girls had not seen it since the inundation. A few trees that had bent before the wave and not broken reared their heads against the blue sky. The undergrowth had flourished in the increased sunlight so that the island was clothed in green. New young trees had been planted lavishly and all the debris had been cleared away and burned.

What caught the eye however was the house which, majestic and solid, dominated the island. They had known exactly what it was like from the plans and drawings. They knew the exact size and shape of all the rooms, the furniture for which they had purchased with such care and thought and which they would now have the pleasure of seeing *in situ*. But none of this knowledge did justice to the reality. It was built of large blocks of green-tinted stone and consisted of a square tower two stories high. The rooms were built round a central enclosed courtyard, in the center of which a tinkling fountain played. Two single-story wings extended from either side of the central building.

The front door was of massive iron-studded oak. The windows had Spanish-type balconies of delicate wrought iron and were protected by iron grilles. The house was set in a grove of young fruit trees of every variety that would grow in the almost perfect climate. The three of them went ashore first and were met by the engineer who had remained behind to go over the equipment with them. They wandered through the spacious rooms and explored the courtyard, the greater part of which was always in welcome shade. The east wing was divided into apartments for the servants, while the west wing was retained for the machinery.

They walked to the center of the island where the cave had been reroofed with a massive reinforced concrete dome. They sank underground in a small elevator and gazed at the humming machinery. A powerful furnace supplied by the highly inflammable and inexhaustible gas was producing high-pressure steam which passed through pipes to a turbine. The revolving blades of the turbine spun a shaft coupled to the rotor of the generator and the rapid rotation of the rotor generated electricity in the windup of the stator. At the moment it was just ticking over, producing enough power for domestic use only. When the broadcasting machine was installed it could be increased to produce whatever power was required. Syn was fascinated and stayed behind with the engineer while Triton and Vinca returned to their guests.

The ensuing weeks were busy and everyone helped move in the furniture and equipment.

Nero, Hercules, Avon and Caesar worked hard and Captain McPherson, Mr. Greenway and Triton also lent a hand, while the engineer helped Dr. Cunningham with his machine and was very curious as to its function.

When Triton had first designed this house he had anticipated that all the machinery would be housed in the west wing. The engineers had pointed out that it would be far better to have the generating equipment in the cave, which was supplied with both gas and water. It would also prevent noise in the house itself and it was a simple matter to run in a cable.

He had not realized the computer would be so small and the result was that the west wing now only contained the broadcasting machine and looked very empty.

In due course everything was moved in, but it would be weeks before it was arranged satisfactorily. They were glad of the almost vacant west wing which became stacked with crates of all sizes. Meanwhile everyone lived on the ship and they kept in contact with world news by radio.

The political situation was deteriorating. Russia had helped China with war material as well as giving her moral support and the latter was steadily pressing forward into India. Fighting was severe and extended along the whole front. The sympathy of the West lay with India and she received war material from both Britain and America.

When China was fully committed in men and materials Russia without warning suddenly invaded her. She had weakened the giant to the best of her ability and now thrust at her across the Mongolian border with maximum strength. The Mongolian Peoples Republic is a large sparsely populated country to the north of China. Its 600,000 square miles support a population of 1,050,000, less than two people per square mile.

Membership in the Communist block had brought Outer Mongolia rich rewards in aid, especially from the Soviet Union. Whether Russia brought political pressure to bear in view of her massive aid or simply took what she wanted is not known. Using the Transmongolian railway, however, she poured a highly mechanized army across the border, which cut like a scythe deep into China's side. In spite of the lessons of history she anticipated a quick victory. Invasion of a homeland produces a strong response on the biological level. Basic territorial defense is a genetic attribute of the human species and invasion of home territory immediately produces a powerful and cooperative resistance on the instinctive level.

China recoiled at such a mighty blow but rode it and responded with the same surge of nationalism that Russia herself had experienced when invaded by Nazi Germany. Factions, quarrels and misunderstandings ceased at this violation of her national sovereignty and China for the first time in generations became fully united.

At one stroke Russia achieved what Chinese politicians had failed to do and had given up hope of ever accomplishing. Russia silenced China's inner conflicts and liberated a shackled giant. The hordes of China behaved like killer ants on the march and like them could not be stopped. The dramatic Russian advance imperceptibly slowed down and their numbers gradually diminished. Many of the Chinese were literally unarmed and the loss of life was frightful. Even so, the horrifying casualties made only a dent in the total Chinese population.

Meanwhile war was escalating and slowly becoming world-wide. Everyone feared atomic attack but the warring nations confined themselves to conventional weapons. The danger would come when one nation was obviously going to be the loser unless she tried to snatch victory from defeat by using the atom.

chapter thirteen

〜〜〜〜〜〜

THE NEWS BULLETINS of various countries were listened to regularly and although they were depressing they hardly seemed real on this peaceful tropical island. The blue sea stretched to the horizon in every direction, and on the sand by the lagoon, or by the newly planted fruit trees with the sun shining out of a cloudless sky, it was difficult to think of armies locked in mortal combat. When Triton and the girls were in their natural habitat gliding between coral reefs or drifting silently in the warm transparent shallows it was impossible. In that magic colored world which excluded all sound from the upper air, the mental picture conjured up by the news of sweating, toiling, weary men destroying each other was washed completely away. It was necessary to walk again upon the land before such images could return.

Dr. Cunningham connected his machine to the cable from the powerhouse and started it broadcasting. It stood firm and still, its steady vibration only detectable when touched by the hand, and once more the *Poseidon* was fully powered. The duplicate machines and spares were stored in the west wing, though hidden from view now by innumerable crates and boxes of various shapes and sizes. The last equipment to be brought ashore was the two helicopters, which even with the help available were difficult to move. They were eventually placed in a hangar built for them behind the west wing of the house. They were specially designed to fly on broadcast power and were an improvement on the original plane that Triton had flown across the Atlantic from Scotland.

At last the holds were empty and a celebration dinner party was held in the dining room of Sea Mount. Crockery and china were borrowed from the ship as the household equipment was not yet all unpacked. It was a merry meal which everyone enjoyed. The following days were busy and everyone was engaged in unpacking boxes of china and glass, washing them and putting them away. Curtains were brought out, pressed and hung up. Furniture was uncrated and taken to various rooms. Everyone joined in and Triton realized that his guests, including Captain McPherson and Mr. Greenway, were working very hard indeed.

He had a word with them about it but none of them felt inclined to laze about while others worked, and Triton found the situation embarrassing. He had not invited the Cunninghams on this trip to make them work; neither of them were as young as the others, and the weather was hot. He realized that as long as everyone else was busy they felt they must give a hand.

Syn and Vinca worked hard from dawn to dusk and were thoroughly enjoying themselves. They took the help of the nearest person without giving it a thought.

Triton solved the dilemma by ordering McPherson to New York to buy provisions and suggested that the Cunninghams take the opportunity of seeing that city. They were both delighted. The ship was to go straight to New York, drop the American engineer and load up with stores so they would be independent of outside food for a long time to come. On the way back they would stop at St. Vincent and pick up the families of the crew and bring them back to their new homes.

The next day they watched the *Poseidon* nose out of the lagoon under power and when free of the coral reef spread her wings and set course for America. They waved to their friends until they could no longer see them. The three returned to the house, the girls chatting merrily. They would be alone on the island until the ship returned.

The distance to New York was about two thousand miles which the *Poseidon* should be able to cover easily in ten days. Say two weeks going, allowing for bad weather, two weeks back, and a stay of one week. Triton considered they should see her again in five or six weeks. They woke early and worked in the house, retreating into the sea during the heat of the day and not reappearing until the cool of the evening. They reveled in their return to home waters. The dolphins were glad to see them, and word passed round the herds that Triton was back with his two companions. Many of them came to see him from other herds out of curiosity, something that had never happened before. Triton did not realize it but he was acquiring a reputation in his undersea world. He tore through the sea with a girl on either side of him reveling in speed. They hunted with the dolphins, feeding again on food unspoiled by fire. They visited their favorite haunts and grottoes and fed gluttonously on shrimps and lobsters.

Triton kept an eye out for Pussy, his pet octopus, and although he saw several of these weird creatures none of them showed any interest in him—they would view him suspiciously and slither away at his approach.

Twice daily, morning and evening, they listened to the news from England, America, France and Italy, which gave them a good all-round picture of the world situation.

The Russian army, after plunging deep into China, became cut off. Her long lines of communication were severed and this powerful and now isolated force was disintegrated and absorbed by masses of almost unarmed men. As the Russians reported in one of their last communiqués, "When one Chinaman died two others took his place."

Meanwhile China's efforts on the Indian front continued but with less force and thrust than previously, and slowly her advance ground to a halt.

This was the very situation that politicians feared. The crucial moment had arrived when stalemate could be turned into sudden victory by use of the atom. The United Nations' delegates almost walked about with their hands over their ears. Both sides possessed the bomb but neither used it. Instead inexplicable outbreaks of typhoid and bubonic plague broke out almost simultaneously in India and China.

News reports stated that they were mutated and extremely virulent strains and the plague swept through the two nations like a prairie fire. Neither of the invading armies continued to advance in spite of greatly diminished resistance, for they were ravaged in the same way. As the administration lost more and more men organization began to break down and internal confusion spread. Every country clamped shut her borders and sealed herself off as well as she could from the rest of the world and trade virtually ceased.

In this state of affairs rich rewards were to be gained by smuggling and illegal organizations sprang up which traded illicitly in commodities such as food, alcohol and tobacco. This inevitably spread infection in spite of strict precautions by the authorities, who were unable to protect efficiently every mile of their borders.

McPherson kept in contact with Crab Island by radiotelephone. The journey to New York had been uneventful but on arrival they were kept in quarantine. In spite of every nation's efforts the plague spread rapidly over Europe and entered America. The distribution of foodstuffs broke down, and there was rioting and looting. McPherson reported every day and the situation slowly became grimmer.

The men on the *Poseidon* were unable to obtain any stores though at the moment this was no hardship as they had enough on board for several weeks, but what they would do when these were exhausted they did not know. No one was allowed off the ship, except the American engineer. The news bulletins from Europe became more and more apprehensive as country after country fell victim, undoubtedly partly due to wholesale smuggling. The death penalty was invoked for this crime by every country in the world and there was a wave of summary executions which slowed but did not stop the illicit trade.

The greed for profit was even greater than the fear of death, and as conditions became worse the financial rewards of smuggling reached gigantic proportions. The breakdown of distribution facilities caused famine as country after country in Europe became decimated by the plague. The disposal of the dead became an administrative problem, and mass burials began to take place.

The war in India practically stopped with only sporadic bursts of gunfire from the opposing sides. It became obvious that the world outbreak of typhoid and bubonic plague was the outcome of bacterial warfare though who started it was uncertain.

The last country to become a victim was England. If she could have stopped all shipping entering her ports she might have remained immune. The realistic Prime Minister spoke to the nation on television and presented the problem bluntly and brutally. "If we cut off all communication with the outside world we have a chance of escaping the plague," he said, "but we will still have to pay a heavy toll. We will not be able to support our population and many will die of starvation. This however would be a cleaner death, and self-limiting. If we do not have the fortitude to do this we can import both food and plague which might wipe out every man, woman and child in the land." He proposed taking the former action and all ports and airfields would be sealed until the plague was over or the government changed. He was a man of great personality and carried the nation with him until starvation stalked the streets. The army and navy guarded the shores of Britain but the plague arrived. No smugglers were caught but many people believed this to be the cause. Finding a nation weakened by starvation nobly born, the plague ripped through the land destroying right and left.

Triton and the girls listened to the last news broadcast by the B.B.C. The B.B.C. apologized for this unprecedented break in transmission which was due to lack of sufficient technical staff to operate the equipment. This failure was due to circumstances which were beyond their control.

It was the last transmission ever heard from England. Somehow the statement framed in this particular way struck the three of them to the heart. Now, when it was impossible to do anything, they agonized about those they knew and loved in London. What was happening to Vicky and Jack Crane, Triton wondered, and whipped himself with remorse for not having asked them to come on the trip. Vicky, he knew, had wanted to come and it was only to avoid possible complications that he had not asked her. Even with his excessive modesty he suspected she might be falling in love with him and he had no wish to hurt her.

London must be a ghastly sight and the whole world had become a charnelhouse. He lost his appetite for food at the thought of the millions dying of starvation until both the girls became worried about him.

They were young and resilient and had known civilization such a short time that what was happening only had the substance of a dream. When they were not listening to the news they forgot about it—for which Triton was thankful.

Grief for the follies of the human race would help

no one and they were both too young for sadness. France and Italy ceased transmission and eventually all the continental wave bands became silent. They continued to listen to American broadcasts although these were depressing, listing as they did nothing but catastrophes such as the ever-mounting death rate and the increase in looting and civil rioting. Fires broke out every day in the big cities and a rapidly depleting fire service would soon be unable to cope with them. Mankind was not dying gracefully. They kept in daily contact with McPherson who phoned every evening and they were always waiting anxiously at the time he was due.

"*Poseidon* calling—can you hear me?"

"Yes, Triton speaking."

Syn had rigged up a loudspeaker so they could all hear.

"Dr. and Mrs. Cunningham have suddenly become ill, with headaches and a high temperature."

"What's the doctor say?"

McPherson laughed.

"Half New York is dying. I've tried to get one but there's not a hope."

"What are you doing, Mac?"

"Giving them aspirin and plenty of fluids. Your boys are looking after them very well."

"How are you keeping?"

"I'm well enough, touch wood, and there's plenty of that around."

"Look after yourself, Mac."

"Is that you, Vinca?"

"Yes."

"Thought I recognized your voice. You and Syn well?"

"Yes, Mac, we're all well, but wish you were with us," said Syn.

"Don't we all," said McPherson dryly.

"I'll ring the same time tomorrow—goodbye."

"Goodbye, Mac."

"*Poseidon* calling."

"Triton here—what's the news."

"Bad, I fear. They're both delirious and have lumps under their arms. It's the plague all right."

"I wish I could help you, Mac," said Triton somberly.

"I'm glad you three are not here—all the world seems to be dying."

"How are the boys?" said Syn.

There was a short pause.

"They're doing all right except for Nero—he has a high fever but won't go to bed."

"Tell him he's got to, from me," said Vinca.

McPherson chuckled.

"I'll do that Vinca—must sign off now, someone's calling. Same time tomorrow—goodbye."

Vinca burst into tears.

"What's going to happen to them?" she sobbed.

Syn put her arms round her sister, but could think of nothing to say.

"I wish I'd never sent them to New York," muttered Triton.

He seemed to be killing all his friends either by inaction or action. If he had only asked Vicky and Jack Crane to come on the trip, and not sent

McPherson and the Cunninghams to New York, they would all be here safe and well.

"*Poseidon* calling—are you there?"

"We can hear you but you are very faint," answered Triton.

"I feel it. The Cunninghams are dead and everyone else has gone down with the same thing."

The sound of vomiting came over the loudspeaker.

"Sorry—couldn't help that—don't feel so good myself."

Vinca and Syn began to cry.

"Lie down, Mac, and take some aspirin."

"I'll do that. Can I hear you girls crying?" he asked.

"Not really," said Syn in a shaky voice.

"It's no good doing that. I've had a good life and enjoyed it—which everyone can't say. I was coming toward the end anyway. Thank God you're safe and sound where you are." There was a pause and they could hear McPherson being sick again. After a moment he spoke again.

"New York is almost hidden by smoke—there must be fires everywhere."

"How are the boys, Mac?" asked Triton.

"It's hard to say, they're just curled up in their bunks in silence."

Again there was the sound of vomiting.

"I must sign off and lie down. I'll try and phone you tomorrow if I can make it. The best of luck to you all." There was a click as he switched off.

Triton sat there in stony silence, while the girls

sobbed in each other's arms. This time it was their own world that was dying. They had known Captain McPherson, Nero, Avon, Caesar and Hercules ever since they could remember and the thought of them dying struck home in a way that the death of nations could not.

Triton sat staring blankly, wishing he could alter the past. All three were waiting anxiously for McPherson's next call but the time came and went. In spite of repeated attempts on Triton's part, the *Poseidon* remained silent and they never again made contact with her.

Triton could not get McPherson out of his mind. He kept thinking of the man dying alone and unaided on board the *Poseidon*. He felt as if he had killed the Cunninghams too but at least he could console himself with the thought that if they had not come on the trip they would almost certainly have died in Scotland. He grieved for Nero, Avon, Caesar and Hercules who had served him so faithfully and so well.

If only the authorities had not detained the *Poseidon,* all might have been well. She had been held, like all incoming vessels, as a result of legislation rapidly enacted in an attempt to control smuggling. The tragedy was that the procedure continued when it was no longer of any value.

Sporadic news broadcasts continued from America for some weeks until, one by one, they stopped. Eventually the ether was silent—all transmission on earth had ceased. Toward the end, either in desperation or by mistake, someone had pushed a button somewhere and a new type of atomic bomb exploded fruitlessly between Rome and Cassino. World communications having ceased, the remnants of dying humanity never knew of this last futile outrage against nature.

chapter 14

TIME DIMINISHED and eventually healed their grief and sorrow. The three of them slipped back naturally into their underwater way of life. Triton allowed the eating of nothing but sea food in case of contamination, not knowing how typhoid and plague were spread. It eventually occurred to him that it was an opportunity to test the computer. Syn sat down at the keyboard.

"Medical Department, please."

The machine typed back: "At your service, what do you wish to know?"

"What is the plague?"

They watched as the answer was rapidly typed back: "A specific infectious disease caused by *B. pestis.*"

She looked questioningly at Triton.

"Ask how it's spread."

She did so and the machine answered: "Principal factors are briefly as follows.

"1. Disease primarily affects rats.

"2. Rat fleas suck blood containing bacilli.

"3. Rat fleas attack man and inoculate him when biting.

"4. Spread among rats is due to rat fleas, cannibalization and possibly human feces and infected food.

"5. From rat to man infection is solely by fleas. Infection is rarely from man to man. Spread of epidemic is practically entirely due to spread in rats and thence to each human being individually. Drinking water apparently of no influence.

"6. Epidemic is always preceded by epizootic disease in rats or rarely other ground animals—i.e., ground squirrel in Californian epidemic. Outbreak in animals in a district precedes human infection by two weeks."

"What does epizootic mean?" asked Vinca.

Syn typed the question, as none of them had heard the word before.

"Question not understood," answered the computer.

"It's using words it doesn't know," said Vinca indignantly.

Triton laughed.

"We're not communicating with an intelligence. Ask for the Dictionary."

Syn did so and repeated the question which was immediately answered.

"Epizootic—widespread disease among the lower animals."

"We can eat what we like then," said Syn turning to Triton.

"We'd better check on typhoid first," he said. They did so and found it was spread by fingers, food and flies. Outbreaks had been traced to contaminated milk and water supplies. As none of this was possible they felt free to eat anything that grew on the island, as well as in the sea.

Both girls were relieved for although they were quite happy eating natural seafood and often preferred it, they had also acquired a taste for human cooking. They had a large collection of cookery books and were looking forward to experimenting in the kitchen and producing exotic dishes.

They had been busy in the house all the morning and as usual they made for the sea, where they would lunch on prawn or lobster and remain during the heat of the day. Vinca and Triton were amazed when Syn decided not to come.

"I'm not hungry. I think I'll sit in the shade," she said.

"It'll be cooler with us than up here," said Vinca.

"I want to read," she answered.

When they had gone Syn wandered round the house. Unable to make up her mind what to do she chose one or two books at random but they did not hold her interest.

It was hot in the house and wiping the perspiration from her face she relaxed in the courtyard. The noise of the fountain was pleasant. She opened the book she had brought but put it down after a few minutes. She could not concentrate and it made no sense.

She lay back and shivered, feeling chilly in the shade. She returned to the house and going up to the bedroom, washed her hands and face and lay down on the bed.

It was here in the cool of the evening that Triton and Vinca found her. She was tossing restlessly in her sleep and there was a fine perspiration on her face. They looked at her anxiously and Triton asked Vinca for a towel. He sat on the bed and gently wiped Syn's face. Opening her eyes she smiled weakly and putting out her hand grimaced with pain.

"What's the matter, Syn?"

"It hurts," she mumbled.

"Where does it hurt, my dear?"

Her eyes closed and she did not answer.

"Where does it hurt, Syn?"

"Under my arm," she muttered apparently half asleep.

Triton felt his blood turn to water and his tongue dry up in his mouth. He tried to swallow without saliva, and heard Vinca's gasp behind him. He looked at Syn's flushed face, and the fine beads of sweat along her hairline. It was impossible for the plague to reach them here. He lifted her arm gently and felt the telltale swelling in her armpit. No, his mind screamed, no—not Syn. Vinca was sobbing quietly and persistently and with an effort he controlled himself. Both the Cunninghams had lumps under their arms before they died; McPherson had told him so. He had heard them referred to often enough over the air during the last dreadful days. Now Syn had one. His breath caught in his throat and he prevented himself with difficulty from weeping. He wiped her face again tenderly and she mumbled something in her sleep. He rose and taking Vinca by the arm led her gently from the room.

"You mustn't let her hear you crying."

Vinca clutched his arm.

"Is it the plague—is it?" she asked desperately.

"We'll try and find out from the computer but

first of all we must give her some aspirin and fluids. Where's the medicine chest?"

Vinca dried her eyes.

"It's not unpacked yet but I know where it is."

They hurried down to the west wing and Triton opened the crate which was packed full of antibiotics and other medicines. He removed a typewritten leaflet on top and searched through the various cartons until he found what he wanted. They returned to the bedroom and lifting up Syn's head he made her swallow three aspirins and drink a glass of water. She was shivering a little and between them they took off her clothes and put her between the sheets, where she fell into an uneasy sleep.

"You watch her while I go down to the computer."

Vinca nodded and pulled a chair up beside the bed.

Triton hurried downstairs but his laborious typing was too slow and he returned for Vinca. Syn was sleeping and they crept out of the room and hurried downstairs.

"Ask for the signs of bubonic plague!"

Vinca typed rapidly and the answer came back.

"Question not understood."

Triton swore.

"Ask for the Medical Department," he said and Vinca did so.

"At your service, what do you wish to know?"

Vinca needed no prompting and typed their question rapidly. The machine answered at length.

"The signs of bubonic plague are as follows—

"Sudden onset, chill, headache, restlessness, rapid pulse and respiration, high fever; symptoms often fully developed in a few hours. Bubo—swelling size of egg in armpits or groins—very tender, edema may be extensive."

The machine went on typing while they gazed at each other in consternation.

"We'll take her temperature and pulse," said Triton and they returned upstairs. Syn's pulse was 95 and her temperature 103° and they looked at each other fearfully. They needed little sleep and watched her carefully throughout the night, having ascertained from the computer they possessed no specific treatment.

In the early hours of the morning Triton went downstairs to make some tea and while the kettle was boiling he returned to the chest of medicines. Among all these modern drugs surely there was something that could help her he thought. He noticed the leaflet and picked it up. The first paragraph caught his attention: "Although there are many diseases there are comparatively few symptoms and physical signs. It is therefore easy to make an incorrect diagnosis. Before you attempt to do this study the differential diagnosis of each symptom."

Triton read it through again carefully and hopefully. Could they be mistaken? Syn had all the symptoms of plague. Fever, raised pulse rate, restlessness, and the feared bubo—the typical swellings that occurred in axillae and groins of plague victims. He hurried to the computer and typed slowly asking for the Dictionary.

"At your service, what do you wish to know?"

"The meaning of differential diagnosis?"

The machine typed rapidly: "Differential diagnosis

means: 'Distinguishing between two diseases of a similar character by comparing their symptoms.' "

Triton sat still, his brow furrowed in thought. The answer did not seem to help much. He read the answer again carefully.

"Difference between two diseases," he muttered and glanced again at the leaflet and read the last phrase aloud: "Differential diagnosis of each symptom."

He typed another question.

"What are the causes of swelling under one arm?"

The machine began to chatter, typing almost faster than he could read: "The three main causes for enlargement of the glands in one axilla without enlargement of the glands elsewhere are as follows:

"1. Septic absorption from sore place upon the fingers, arms, breast, shoulders or upper part of back. Sometimes the source of septic absorption is by no means obvious, it may be no more than a slight scratch. Inflammatory glands are painful and associated with a fever and red streaks are sometimes visible on the skin extending from inflammatory source.

"2. Secondary deposits of carcinoma from the breast. Breast should be palpated carefully for unsuspected lump; no fever or malaise.

"3. Tuberculous axillary glands have been recorded but are uncommon without involving those in the neck.

"4. Lymphadenoma (Hodgkin's disease). Other lymphatic glands will presently become enlarged."

The typing stopped. There was no mention of the bubo of bubonic plague, Triton noticed with surprise. He read the answer again carefully and then raced upstairs taking the steps two at a time, Vinca looked up as he entered the room.

"She's awake."

He looked at Syn who was lying quiet but flushed. He walked over and looked down at her anxiously.

"How're you feeling?"

"My arm hurts and I'm sweating and need a bath."

Triton smiled.

"Have you injured or grazed yourself anywhere in the last few days?"

She shook her head, and his hopes sank.

"I want to have a look at you," and she obediently let Vinca remove her nightgown. She lay back, golden brown against the white linen sheets. Her breasts were small and pear-shaped and he felt them carefully. They were firm and to his relief he could feel no lump. He carefully examined her right hand and arm. On the inner surface just above the wrist and traveling nearly up to the elbow he saw some red streaks which were tender to pressure. He turned her hand over, and separating the long slender fingers, noticed a partially healed scratch on her thumb.

"You've scratched your thumb," he said with a feeling of relief and hope.

"It's nothing, I don't even remember doing it," Syn said casually.

Triton glanced at Vinca.

"It may be the cause of the swelling under her arm."

A look of hope crossed Vinca's face.

"May it?" she breathed.

"We'll go and find the treatment," he said.

Vinca leapt to her feet and fled downstairs before he had finished speaking.

Triton gave Syn a damp flannel and towel to wipe her face and hands and by the time he joined Vinca she had the answer.

"One capsule of penicillin V.K. 250 mg. every three hours," she said breathlessly.

They searched through the crate and took the carton upstairs and immediately started Syn on the treatment. She responded rapidly and her pulse and temperature fell dramatically. The red streaks on her skin vanished and the lump under her arm became less painful and eventually disappeared. Within a very short time Syn was herself again and the relief was almost too much to bear. Syn was spoiled by them both for a long time—which she thoroughly enjoyed. But Triton did not forget the terror he had felt at the thought of losing her. Quietly he began a course of study in medicine, using the computer and the numerous books they had in their extensive library. He could never become a qualified doctor, but he would at least not be a helpless ignoramus if any of them were to become ill again.

The Triton lay on his back sunbathing. The placid lagoon lapped quietly at his feet and only the occasional cry of a seagull broke the silence of the island. Syn and Vinca, one on either side of him, gazed into the blue vault of the sky, each busy with her own thoughts. The radio had been silent on all wavelengths for a long time and Vinca wondered what it was like in London and what had happened to the vast crowds of people she had seen flooding through its streets.

"Do you think everyone is dead?" she asked speaking her thoughts aloud.

Triton, who was half asleep, grunted and she rolled over on her stomach and looked at him. He lay relaxed and silent and she examined his face closely.

"Do you think everyone is dead?" she murmured.

His hair was gold and his aquiline face a deep bronze. She ran a finger lightly down the strong jaw and Syn rolled over and watched her.

Vinca outlined the dark arched eyebrows.

"I think they look better dark."

Syn nodded.

"He's much better looking than upper-air men," she said thoughtfully.

"Even Antony?" queried Vinca.

Syn colored and nodded her head. "And James?" she asked.

"Of course," said Vinca as she outlined the firmly shaped mouth, but the light touch of her finger on his lips woke him. His blue eyes looked in surprise at the young faces so close to his.

"What are you two doing?" he asked.

"Just admiring you, darling," said Syn.

A faint flush appeared under his bronze.

"I do believe he's blushing," said Vinca with interest.

Triton made an effort to rise, which was a mistake.

Both girls simultaneously seized an arm and hooked a leg over one of his, so that he was pinned down and unable to move.

"I asked you a question," said Vinca kissing him lightly on the mouth.

"Umm, that's rather nice, try it, Syn."

Her sister followed her suggestion and her eyes smiled at Triton as she lifted her head.

He was very conscious of their warm young bodies and their kisses were different from any he had experienced.

"What was your question?" he asked desperately.

"Do you think everyone is dead?"

"I think it very likely. Bacterial warfare, especially if mutant strains were used, would be more likely to wipe out humanity than even atomic bombs."

To his astonishment both girls laughed.

"What's funny about that?" he asked indignantly.

"Nothing," said Vinca solemnly.

"It's a terrible tragedy," added Syn seriously.

He looked at their lovely, solemn faces.

"What amuses you, then?"

"You, darling," said Syn kissing him and her soft mouth made him melt.

"We were laughing at your predicament," said Vinca kissing him in her turn.

"My predicament?" he murmured weakly.

"If everyone is dead it will be up to you, darling, won't it?" said Vinca looking at him closely.

"Of course," said Syn in a matter-of-fact voice.

Triton was taken aback at this female pragmatism. He was fearful that humanity might have destroyed itself, but could not bear to think of it, nor had he faced up to the personal implication of such a catastrophe.

He regarded his two charges with a wary eye.

"We don't know what the situation is. All broadcasting has stopped but it need not mean everyone is dead."

"How can we find out?" said Vinca.

"We will ask the dolphins to keep a lookout for man, both at sea and on the coasts. They will pass the word on from one to another so that a man will not be able to sail on the sea or walk on a beach without us knowing."

They rose to their feet enthusiastically.

"An excellent idea," said Vinca.

"We'll tell them now," added Syn.

He watched them race into the water and vanish. The ripples of their passage passed leaving the surface of the lagoon calm and unruffled. They were beautiful creatures in character as well as in appearance, he reflected, and he wondered if the three of them were the last of the human race, and devoutly hoped not. None of them would leave the island for a long time to come, whatever the dolphins reported. He had no intention of risking the frightful epidemic which must have wiped out the majority of mankind if not all. But eventually they would have to find out what had happened to their world.

GREAT MASTERPIECES OF ADULT FANTASY

AVAILABLE IN BALLANTINE BOOKS EDITION

A VOYAGE TO ARCTURUS	David Lindsay
TITUS GROAN—Volume I	Mervyn Peake
GORMENGHAST—Volume II	Mervyn Peake
TITUS ALONE—Volume III	Mervyn Peake
THE WORM OUROBOROS	E. R. Eddison
MISTRESS OF MISTRESSES	E. R. Eddison
A FISH DINNER IN MEMISON	E. R. Eddison
THE MEZENTIAN GATE	E. R. Eddison

and watch for:

THE KING OF ELFLAND'S DAUGHTER	Lord Dunsany
THE WOOD BEYOND THE WORLD	William Morris
THE SILVER STALLION	James Branch Cabell
LILITH	George Macdonald

Uniformly priced at 95¢ each
(Plus 5¢ per book mailing charge)

To order by mail, list the titles you want, add your address with zip code, and enclose $1.00 per title: send to: Dept. CS, Ballantine Books, 36 West 20th Street, New York, New York 10003

The Novels of Edgar Rice Burroughs

(Published in Book Form)

Tarzan Novels

* TARZAN OF THE APES
* THE RETURN OF TARZAN
* THE BEASTS OF TARZAN
* THE SON OF TARZAN
* TARZAN AND THE JEWELS OF OPAR
* JUNGLE TALES OF TARZAN
* TARZAN THE UNTAMED
* TARZAN THE TERRIBLE
* TARZAN AND THE GOLDEN LION
* TARZAN AND THE ANT MEN
  THE TARZAN TWINS (juvenile)
* TARZAN, LORD OF THE JUNGLE
* TARZAN AND THE LOST EMPIRE
* TARZAN AT THE EARTH'S CORE
* TARZAN THE INVINCIBLE
* TARZAN TRIUMPHANT
* TARZAN AND THE CITY OF GOLD
* TARZAN AND THE LION MAN
* TARZAN AND THE LEOPARD MEN
* TARZAN'S QUEST
* TARZAN AND THE FORBIDDEN CITY
* TARZAN THE MAGNIFICENT
* TARZAN AND "THE FOREIGN LEGION"
  TARZAN AND THE TARZAN TWINS (juvenile)
* TARZAN AND THE MADMAN
* TARZAN AND THE CASTAWAYS

Other Novels (Unrelated to one another)

* THE MUCKER
  THE GIRL FROM HOLLYWOOD
  THE LAND THAT TIME FORGOT
  THE CAVE GIRL
  THE BANDIT OF HELL'S BEND
  THE ETERNAL LOVER
  THE MOON MAID (Moon Men)
  THE MAD KING
  THE OUTLAW OF TORN

THE MONSTER MEN

JUNGLE GIRL
THE OAKDALE AFFAIR AND THE RIDER
* THE LAD AND THE LION
THE DEPUTY SHERIFF OF COMANCHE COUNTY
TALES OF THREE PLANETS

Martian Novels

* A PRINCESS OF MARS
* THE GODS OF MARS
* THE WARLORD OF MARS
* THUVIA, MAID OF MARS
* THE CHESSMEN OF MARS
* THE MASTER MIND OF MARS
* A FIGHTING MAN OF MARS
* SWORDS OF MARS
* SYNTHETIC MEN OF MARS
* LLANA OF GATHOL
* JOHN CARTER OF MARS

Apache Novels

* THE WAR CHIEF
* APACHE DEVIL

Inner-World Novels

AT THE EARTH'S CORE
PELLUCIDAR
TANAR OF PELLUCIDAR
TARZAN AT THE EARTH'S CORE
BACK TO THE STONE AGE
LAND OF TERROR
SAVAGE PELLUCIDAR

Venus Novels

PIRATES OF VENUS
LOST ON VENUS
CARSON ON VENUS
ESCAPE ON VENUS

* Available in 50¢ Authorized Editions from Dept. CS, Ballantine Books, Inc., 101 Fifth Ave., New York, N. Y. 10003. (Please add 5¢ per book postage on orders for less than 4 books.)

The great masterpieces of fantasy by
J. R. R. TOLKIEN

The Hobbit

and

The Lord of the Rings

Part I—THE FELLOWSHIP OF THE RING

Part II—THE TWO TOWERS

Part III—THE RETURN OF THE KING

plus

The Tolkien Reader

Smith of Wootton Major and Farmer Giles of Ham

The Road Goes Ever On: A Song Cycle
(music by Donald Swann)

Note: These are the complete and authorized paper-bound editions, published only by Ballantine Books.

To order by mail, send $1.00 for each book (except for *The Road Goes Ever On* which requires $3.00) to Dept. CS, Ballantine Books, 101 Fifth Avenue, New York, N.Y. 10003.

**In Science Fiction
Ballantine Books Brings You
the Best of the Established Authors
and the Most Exciting New Writers**

⎼⎼⎼⎼⎼⎼⎼⎼⎼⎼⎼⎼⎼⎼⎼

◆

Send price of book plus 5¢ a copy for postage to
Dept. CS, BALLANTINE BOOKS, INC., 101
Fifth Avenue, New York, New York 10003, with
your name, address and ZIP CODE NUMBER.